Y0-DNL-540

Pigs
When They Straddle
the Air

A Novel in
Seven Stories

Julie J.
Nichols

"THESE STORIES INVITE US TO BREAK GRAND CONCEPTS down to the relational and minute. We are asked to ponder human circumstance, history, and, best of all, potential. The calculus of love and coexistence, the book suggests, never reaches an ultimate tally. As readers, we are required to suspend sweeping moral judgment as events unfold for one of the most warmly unsentimental and incisive definitions of family I have ever read.

"The language is sharp and sometimes wildly funny, and the story resides in a universe of equal-opportunity access to mystery. True healing forces, in this narrative, do not compete. Rather, they combine and collaborate, at least when they are most efficacious. Within the first few pages, I was not only willing, but delighted, to suspend my own (painful) cynicism and simply follow the mystical premises of the story to their beautiful destinations. In that way, reading the narrative was a kind of healing sequence—it's a retreat, a sacred space for reconsideration and reflection."

—Karin Anderson, author of *breach: a narrative*

"JUST AS GOD'S EYE IS ON THE SPARROW, JULIE NICHOLS'S clear-sighted, penetrating eye is on the lives of Mormon women and men and our yearnings and shortcomings. This memorable collection of finely crafted stories helps us see both ourselves and our world better and feel seen by one of our own. Nichols is an important, unfailing talent whose work as a writer and teacher of writers blesses our community."

—Joanna Brooks, author of *Book of Mormon Girl*

"THESE LINKED STORIES, UNLIKE THE MASS OF MORMON fiction, blend insider and outsider perspectives—warp and weft of a tight weave. They are consistently faithful and questioning, intelligent and spiritual, essentially Mormon and essentially inclusive of those who inhabit the fringe. Ethically sound, each story has a narrator who is harmless as a dove and wise as a

serpent. Through this alchemy of opposites, the reader is borne to the edge of mystery, to a condition of 'puzzlement and love.'"
—John Bennion, writing professor at BYU, author of *Breeding Leah and Other Stories* and *Falling Toward Heaven*

"NICHOLS IS ONE OF THOSE RARE WRITERS WHO UNDERstands the complexity of faith: the way it can haunt as well as enchant and its potential to hurt as well as heal. In this intricately patterned collection, she addresses the violence, mystery, and most of all the messy beauty of marriage, motherhood, love, and forgiveness in a lush, lyrical prose which honours the magical in the everyday."
—Jenn Ashworth, author of *The Friday Gospels*

"IN HER MULTIGENERATIONAL, DEBUT COLLECTION OF short stories, Julie Nichols explores the changes in personal relationships and in the LDS Church in Salt Lake City, Utah, over four decades. This collection, which can also be read as a novel, delves into issues often ignored and avoided by LDS families and their culture and offers both insights and empathy. Through these stories, Nichols makes an open and invaluable contribution to the ongoing dialogue surrounding the many much-needed transformations."
—Sue Booth-Forbes, director,
Anam Cara Writer's and Artist's Retreat, Ireland

Pigs
When They
Straddle the Air

A Novel in Seven Stories by

Julie J. Nichols

ZARAHEMLA BOOKS

"Pennyroyal, Cohosh, Rue," first published in *Sunstone* 12:3 May 1988; rep in *Catalyst* Summer 1989 and in *With Child*, ed. Marni Asplund-Campbell (Signature, 1998)

"Without Number" published in *Dialogue*, winter 2006

"Fifth Element" published in *Sunstone* December 1997 (20:8) (1st place winner, D.K. Brown fiction contest)

"Pigs When They Straddle the Air" in the *Provo-Orem Word*, August 2010

"Seven Times One," the poem in "Fifth Element," by Jean Ingelow (1820–1897), is in the public domain.

Roland Alder's methods and sayings in "Everything To Do With You" are adapted by permission from the teachings of Lansing Barrett Gresham, founder of Integrated Awareness™ (http://inawareness.com/).

Cover images by Corinne Geertsen (corinnegeertsen.org)
Cover design by Jason Robinson
Design and layout by Marny K. Parkin

ISBN 978-0-9883233-5-3

Printed in the U.S.A.

Published by:
Zarahemla Books
869 East 2680 North
Provo, UT 84604
info@zarahemlabooks.com
ZarahemlaBooks.com

To the family.
God bless us, every one!

Contents

Cast of Characters

Annie (V. Annie MacDougal) b. 1970

Riva Maynard, a Mormon feminist b. approx. 1956

Nina ———, Riva's eventual partner.

Katie Maynard, b. 1979, daughter of Riva.

Paul Maynard, b. approx. 1952. Riva's husband at one time, married approximately 1976.

Grandma Jean, grandmother of Paul, b. approximately 1888.

Suzanne, Paul's sister, b. approx. 1955.

Adela Suaros, friend and colleague of Riva.

Carlos Suaros, Adela's husband.

Sean Finn, b. approx. 1978, neglected son of Savin' Sam Finn, an itinerant non-LDS preacher.

The Lubbocks: Kiefer, his wives Jean and Peggy, and their children, in particular Sarah Eileen aka Leeny, b. approximately 1992.

Roland Alder, a charismatic healer from northern California, teacher incidentally of Suzanne, more seriously of Riva and also Annie.

Garrett, Katie's son, b. 1997

SETTING: Neighborhoods on the east side of Salt Lake City, Utah, and canyons in the mountains east of cities on Utah's Wasatch Front.

The Fifth Element

1987

THE WOMEN BEHIND HOSPITAL DESKS ARE TRAINED IN ICE.
They reassure me not at all. I have tried thinking of the stars over
camp, the backlit faces of my girls at evening fire, the feel and scent
of dry pine needles in dust under my feet, but I'm not comforted. I
long for the hands of my friends extended to save me, as if it were
I battling the shallow rapids of the Snake where it runs past Jordan
Camp, as if it were Riva extending herself to me from land, pulling
me safely home. I press my hands into my forehead, where the stuff
of my brain feels unprotected, soft, spilling upward into the night.
I think of the hands of my friends on my head and I want to crush
myself into them, reshaped and reformed, forgiven for letting this
happen—forgiven for letting Katie go.

I WAS NAMED AFTER MY MOTHER, VERA ANN. V. ANNIE
Macdougal. I took this job to earn money, of course, but also
to make the break with her once and for all, out in the open, up
front, as if it hadn't been made years ago in *my* mind. I know
plenty of women my age who are reconciled with their mothers, with the idea of Mother: Bitty Seamons broke every crystal
goblet and Noritake serving piece in her mother's china cabinet
when she was fifteen in a fit of fury because her mother wouldn't
let her date Rob Kendall yet, but she married him in the Mormon temple a year ago and her mother is busy tying quilts for
the baby that's due next month, proud to be a grandmother at
last. Renee Malton ran away from home once all the way to Reno,
but now she's at the Community College, like me living at home,

but unlike me going shopping with her mother as if they were the same age, laughing and giggling and having lunch at the mall like peers. Patrice Chenard, too—when her mother put her in that school for "troubled teens" I thought she'd never speak to her again. But now she sides with her mother on the issue of her younger sister, Collie, who's one of the most active dealers of the drugs kids should say no to at Lincoln Junior High.

It's clear to me now that the glitches in my friends' mother-daughter relations were only diversions. Those forays into rage and destruction never meant anything. Should I, I wonder, have sabotaged my mother's life work, erased the files on her computer, written a scathing expose of my mother's life (what would I have said? She's the salt of the earth), and published it anonymously in the *Trib* for everyone to see? Then would my head be clear now, this gaping hole filled in forever by the clean expression of my childish wrath?

But I never thought to erase my mother's files. She writes recipes for the national press. Tomato pies, hot pickles, whole wheat cinnamon rolls, soufflés with zucchini and celery. Her food is wholesome, inexpensive, quick to fix, above all delicious, calculated to earn a fame acceptable to Mormon mothers. Another daughter might have joined her enterprise enthusiastically, brilliantly. But the sets of our literary leanings—my *logos* and hers—never intersected. From the beginning I loved poems more than God.

Even when I was seven I knew that the lists of ingredients and measurements on her typewriter platen were sacred to her in some way analogous to the way certain poems were to me. Once, because I couldn't find any clean paper, I typed a poem I knew, not even one of my own, onto a half-finished recipe card.

"What's this?" she said. "'How sweet is the shepherd's sweet lot'? Where did you hear that?" I showed her the copy of Blake I'd found in the school library. She looked him up, and when she saw that his engravings were sometimes of naked people in copulation, sometimes of angels he said he saw (poor deluded poet), she used her typewriter to write letters that removed him from the district's inventory. Some other mothers rallied around her. My second grade teacher said nothing kind to me when I gave her back the book under duress.

Alone, then, I kept looking for poems I would understand and remember. They were voices humming at me, magnets drawing me to them—spells, maybe. Like a child, I excused my mother for depriving me of my own most sacred words. I thought she simply had different taste. I still don't think her censorship was born of malice, exactly—just a strange kind of protectionism wrongly directed, generated by fear, brought to fruit in the acceptable place of power: the home, the child.

One Sunday my mother woke up with the flu. She had to call the Sunday School people to tell them she wouldn't be able to teach my class as usual. Till I was three she took care of the children in the nursery while other mothers went to their own church classes. Then she taught each of the classes for my age group—four-year-olds, five-year-olds, six. I knew all the right answers about God and Jesus and Joseph Smith, and not another child in the neighborhood had read the Book of Mormon at as young an age as I. All the other mothers were more than willing to let Vera Ann teach us. The fruits of her labor were perfect.

That day my mother had the flu, someone new in the ward found Riva (also new in the ward) to substitute, and Riva brought her woman friend Nina. In my Sunday School class, we were seven-year-olds turning eight. The lessons in the manual provided by the central committee in Salt Lake had titles like "We Will Be Baptized Like Jesus." "Brigham Young was a Great Prophet." "The Pioneers Came Across the Plains." By this time, we'd heard them all officially at least seven times, once during each year of our lives. My mother put up flannel board figures, posters. I don't know who drew the original flannel Moses and Miriam, but the posters—miniatures of which could be found in my Triple Combination—were all by some 1940s artist who seemed not to recognize the noncaucasian origin of the scripture characters. But I didn't know that until later. At seven I only knew that the format for Sunday School was familiar and predictable and, in a mildly irritating way, boring: my mother showing pictures, telling stories brightly, waiting for us to pipe up with the right answers (God help us if we didn't have them by the time we were seven).

So it was a shock, the morning of the flu at our house, to see Riva and Nina sitting there. They wore pants, first of all, which you don't do at church in our corner of Mormondom. I think it's done on the coasts, perhaps, but not where we were. Riva had short curly hair all over her head and Nina's was in braids and she wore overalls. I felt ... interested.

Riva said, first thing, "Do any of you have a favorite story?" Bitty and Robbie and Patricia and Renee stared off into space. There were a couple of other little boys, Billy and somebody else. They stared off into space too. Riva looked at us one at a time but mine were the only eyes she could get to meet hers. I wanted to tell her about my real favorite story, but I knew there was a proper answer, an expected answer. I said, daringly: "The Good Samaritan is a good one" (there was a poster of this that my mother often hung before us in the classroom), "but what I really like is Jabberwocky."

Nina cried out, startling the other children:

> "One, two! One, two! And through and through
>> His vorpal sword went snicker-snack!
> He left it dead, and with its head
>> He went galumphing back!"

"Yes," I said, laughing.

"Come to my arms, my beamish—*girl,*" Nina said. I was too shy to go. Riva carried on with the lesson, about parables in general and the one in the Book of Mormon about the olive tree in particular. But I wasn't finished with these women. I knew I had found a source, a way to replenish and affirm the truth of my own peculiar power, the chant of words, the voice of rhythm making more than the meaning of the sounds.

OTHERS WAITING COME AND GO. A SMALL BOY SCREAMS *over the gash in his leg, and his father, a young, tired gas station attendant by the look of his uniform, holds him, but not close. An old woman presses a handkerchief to her neck, the skin of her arms hanging below her bones like a limp unusable organ. Like the lungs of my Katie-girl, filled with water, the stuff from which once she burst to life and from which she now must suffer. Because I let her go. Because I thought falsely she could handle the river, she said she was unafraid of the river finally, and I believed her. So now I suffer too, I see above me the surface of the water receding even as I reach, even as I strain the roiling white surface shatters me downward and I try to remember the way up, the way up, and my ears and my nose are full and I remember in despair the beautiful emptiness of air but it eludes me in this water and I can't reach it. The work of the water is death.*

TWO WEEKS AFTER THAT SUNDAY WAS THE AUTUMN EQUI-nox. Riva called me on the telephone and said, "Nina and I want you to come to a party with poems and food to celebrate the way the earth is turning." It made sense to me. The earth turns, school starts, we put on warmer clothes and poems repeat the rhythms of this change. It sounded interesting, useful. Anyway I liked Riva and Nina. I'd received a letter from them after that Sunday:

> Dear Annie McDougal: Do you know the one about the moon and the seven-year old girl? Here it is if you don't, because you are seven and you should know.
>
> Love, Riva and Nina

> There's no dew left on the daisies and clover
> There's no rain left in heaven
> I've said my seven times over and over:
> Seven times one are seven.
>
> I am old—so old I can write a letter;
> My birthday lessons are done.
> The lambs play always—they know no better;
> They are only one times one.
>
> O Moon! In the night I have seen you sailing
> And shining so round and low.
> You were bright—ah, bright—but your light is failing:
> You are nothing now but a bow.
>
> You Moon! Have you done something wrong in heaven,
> That God has hidden your face?
> I hope, if you have, you will soon be forgiven,
> And shine again in your place …

There was more, and I still know it by heart. "I am old, you can trust me, linnet, linnet—I am seven times one today." Why has this stayed so long, in my body and in my brain? Is seven truly the magical number so much in myth says it is? Is eight the Mormon age of accountability and baptism due to some subliminal recognition that the deepest rhythms of the first seven years have made their mark and cannot be erased except we be reborn?

I don't know now, and I didn't have the words to think about it then. I said to my mother, "Sister Galsworthy and her friend have invited me to a party, can I go?"

Vera Ann believes in granting the benefit of the doubt until guilt is doubtless. "Some kind of Sunday School party?" she asked. "Certainly, go and have fun."

Nina's house was a square white structure behind Riva's, almost like a playhouse, I thought, or servants' quarters, though Nina was not Riva's servant. Riva's two children and her sometimes-husband made her home look more like ours, with a porch and a fireplace chimney and checkered curtains in the windows and bedrooms upstairs. But Nina's reminded me of the houses of grandmothers, a lone woman's house. The kind of house I wanted for myself: my own small kitchen, my own living room with a rocker and many books, and a bedroom with flowers and cupboards full of the things that made up me.

Or in this case, Nina. I know now what's in those cupboards, the dried verbena and pennyroyal and coriander in jars she throws herself in the fourth room of the house, a room pink with the dust of clay and color-wild on the days she glazes. I know the smell as sandalwood and sage; even when the incense isn't lit, the scent circles the rooms and lifts them off the earth of this town where they're grounded. Vanilla and bayberry candles, next to the cupboard full of wicks and wax by which they're made on certain days of the year; pine, cinnamon, gardenia—light brown, rust, white— these also circle the room, now as they did that day, so that I knew it was no house like I'd ever been in before, and better suited for poems than anyplace I might ever be again.

We sat in the living room, an ordinary brown and white rag rug on the floor, a round small table in the middle, set with flowers—blue cosmos of late summer—and two Shaker chairs and one fine overstuffed green recliner drawn up close. In a miniature fondue pot, potpourri simmered there on the table, a small white candle flickering underneath.

"It's earth, air, fire, and water all at once," Riva said. "The potpourri is the stuff of the earth, simmering in water by the heat of the fire and steaming off into the air. Like it?"

I said I loved it, which I did, though the references to earth and so on meant nothing to me.

"Treasure hunt first thing," said Nina. She handed me the first clue, a quatrain about going outside and looking in the walnut tree and finding a treasure and a pleasure for me. The next clue told me to bring back the shell of a well-eaten walnut, and the rest of the clues were like that: in every hiding place I received a gift from the earth or the air or the water or the fire (Nina's kiln contained bits of throwaway clay), and finally, when my arms were full of value from the elements, we reconvened around the little table in the living room and I placed these offerings on the altar and Riva and Nina took turns reading poems to me about autumn—Keats, Bishop, Dickinson. They named the authors to me so that I would know my colleagues in poetry-making, and when I asked, they helped me memorize the Dickinson: "The morns are meeker than they were ..."

When we had eaten—a spicy pumpkin cake made with whole wheat flour, which I knew my mother would want the recipe for—my new friends asked me if I had any poems of my own to share. No one had ever asked me this before. I promised to bring some next time. I was wild with pleasure: there would be a next time, and I could show my poems.

This was our first ritual, our first party celebrating our own sacred things. In that and in many similar moments over the next two months, without knowing the word "grace," I became a new person. For the first time, I had permission to enjoy publicly what had always been sacred, but never yet named to me. I found it very good.

"I'm afraid of the water, Annie Macdougal," Katie says.

"Afraid?" I can't imagine being afraid: the water, like the earth, is my friend. How many years now have I known the water in all its forms, brought it to the altar, mingled it with air-forms, fire-forms, earth? I even think of skiing as a kind of swimming, a moving through water as crystalline cold, and I celebrate water summer and winter.

"So you can't swim?" I say. "I'll teach you."

I am confident. Teaching little girls seems to be a calling, it comes so easily: stringing beads on a loom in blue and black bird patterns; biscuits on sticks over the Coleman stove; pyramids of kindling and tinder the basis for effective small campfires. Songs—the easiest of all, my favorite to teach, the words first, then I play guitar. I sing to her now: "'Twas grace that taught my heart to fear, and grace my fear relieved ...'" The wrinkle between her eyes eases. She likes these words too. She believes I can help her. She believes in my grace.

THE NEARER I GOT TO EIGHT, THE NEARER NOVEMBER came, the more intensely my mother drove home to us in Sunday School the saving power of the gospel, the importance of baptism by a man who has authority, the new possibility of repentance once we had received the Holy Ghost. I got this not only at Sunday School but at home, too. My father would baptize me—counselor to the bishop, he was, a busy and important man in his business and in our church ward, and I was privileged to have his authority in my house. My mother told me this often. To me, he seemed far away, tall and good-looking but from some other world.

My behavior when he was around differed subtly from my behavior at home without him. When he was at work, I showed respect for recipes, computers, quiet reading, Vera Ann's plans. At Nina's my behavior was different yet again: games outside in the elements, laughter, poems. But for my father, I affected formality, propriety, soberness. These affectations were represented to me as right and proper. No girl-child behaves the same for her father, and sometimes not even for her mother, as she does for her friends. That was the rule I learned. Her father is next to God. She'd better behave as he says.

Halloween morning broke frosty. I wore a black turtleneck and an orange skirt—my mother dressed me classily, put my hair in fashionable twists with ribbons the appropriate colors—and I said to Vera Ann, "Can I take some black-cat cookies to a party at Sister Galsworthy's after school?"

"Didn't you go there day before yesterday?" she said.

"It's an important day," I said. "Halloween."

"When will you go trick-or-treating?"

"After dark," I said. "I'll be home before dinner. Can I take the cookies?" I'd helped make them.

She shook her head. It meant, *well all right, but if you really loved me you wouldn't.* She put six black cats on an orange paper plate decorated with silhouettes of witches. "What's the attraction over there?" she said.

I started to tell her, but then I didn't.

When I got to Nina's in the afternoon, the wind chill had blasted me into winter, even in my black leggings. I drank the rose hip tea she gave me with pleasure. Herb teas, she said, not only warmed you but also gave you health, and I had no compunction about drinking tea in her house, though black tea and coffee were forbidden in our own. "The nutmeg in it will warm you up," she said. "It's full of vitamin C. The sun in a cup."

We did the things we always did: made a potpourri; gathered gifts, representatives of the elements, from the now-dying garden; read poems. Some days we also walked a little way up into the canyon behind the house, but today I had to think of trick-or-treating and being home before dark. Even though we didn't go anywhere, I was late getting home, because Nina showed me some ways to play with my new poems to make them better. I had brought two. Riva shook her head over us. She meant, "You're so remarkable, you makers of poems and pots!" I ran home smiling.

But Vera Ann was furious. "It's six-thirty!" she said. "What can you have been thinking about? What about your piano? Your homework?"

My father was angry too. His placid home life had been disrupted. Vera Ann's recipe-writing had gone sour because of me and had leaked over into their angry childless dinner. He dropped me off at the corner of the next street over and told me to go on by myself while he waited in the car, and hurry. The road was slippery. Frozen drops fell from time to time. I ran from the Chenards' to the Maltons' and slipped in the middle of the street.

In my black witch's robe I suppose I was invisible to my father, who in a flurry of regret turned up the street in his Lincoln as I fell and hit me gently with the right front bumper. I slid twenty feet. The ice and asphalt sliced my leg and arm like glass.

My father, not a man to be hysterical, flung me into the back of his car, and he would have screeched home if the ice had not made him slide silently instead. My mother said, "Will you give her a blessing?" My father said, "Let's take her to the emergency room and see. If we have to we'll call Brother Chenard." You always needed two men for a blessing. That was how it was done.

But at the emergency room he decided I was not seriously enough injured to require a blessing. My left leg required stitches, though, and it hurt. I thought I could remember Nina telling me what herbs soothed pain, and I wanted warm tea, not the fat brown pills the emergency room nurse tried to give me. I asked my mother to call Riva.

She was there with Nina in five minutes. They held my hands. My mother left for a moment to ask a nurse about something, and Nina said, "We're going to give you a blessing." I had no time to say, *my father says there's no need, and you have to have the proper authority anyway, two men, one to pour the oil, one to say the proper words.* Instead they put their hands on my leg, the stitched part of me, and Riva said, "In the name of the Mother and the Father and all that is, we bless you with health and a quick recovery to carry on your pleasure and your work."

From the doorway my father said, "Get out of here," and my mother beside him said, "please," and that, they said later, was why my friends would not be allowed to come to my baptism, even though my leg healed in just a couple of days and it never hurt after that and I went back to school the very next day.

MY BAPTISM WAS TO BE AN EXTENDED-FAMILY CELEBRA-tion. I had no siblings, but I went to the baptisms of every first, second, and third cousin in a two-hundred mile radius to watch them in their white coveralls be immersed in a warm font of water by their fathers or older brothers or uncles, also in white coveralls. They always invited everyone, family, of course. Macdougals cover this state in all their variety and they always play bagpipes and often they sing, one or more of them in groups so practiced they sound professional. Also invited are the bishop of the ward the child lives in and the bishop's counselors, if they want to come; the Sunday School teacher of the child to be baptized, and all his or her Sunday School class, and their parents; and special friends who might not already be in any of these categories.

By special permission I was to be baptized on Thanksgiving morning, so that the traditional after-ceremony meal could be a holiday one attended by all the closely-related Macdougals. Holiday baptisms are not customary and I think my father would have been just as happy if we had done it the old-fashioned way, with all the new eight-year-olds of several wards sitting together at the front of the chapel with their many families filling the pews, and their fathers one by one taking them to stand waist-deep in the font in the proper stance, saying the baptism words as they appear in the Doctrine and Covenants. Usually, too, the after-baptism meals are potluck, but Vera Ann wanted to show off her recipes and my father agreed to show off his home and they took it upon themselves to do all the work.

We planned on forty guests. I went shopping with my mother to seven different stores for the best grocery selections, and to more stores than I could keep track of for the finest white baptism dress for me. I wanted to quote something to my mother about "in all her finery, hee hee!" but I didn't. I had chores to do, tables to set, dishes to place on the elegant tables when the time came. We were all kept very busy.

My mother planned my program. Dobie and Mike Macdougal, the bagpipers, were invited to play "Praise to the Man," a hymn straight from the days of Nauvoo, an old favorite at these affairs because it's perfect for bagpipes (the attribution for this music says "Old Scottish tune") and it honors Joseph Smith. In order to spread around the honor of performing at my baptism, Vera Ann also chose two younger second cousins, who had been baptized in the last year or so, to talk about the Holy Ghost and Jesus. Naturally the entire visiting congregation would sing a song or two together, under the direction of my mother's sister Rayelle, whose clear soprano I had always liked and whose calling in life was to be the chorister for the children's Sunday School in every ward she ever attended.

I said, "Can Riva and Nina speak instead of Lizzie and Ty?"

"Not this time," said Vera Ann.

"I want them to come," I said.

Vera Ann looked angry. "This is for *family*," she said.

RIVA CALLED ME THE NIGHT BEFORE.

"Do you want me and Nina to come to your baptism, Annie Macdougal?" she asked.

"They won't let you," I said.

"Your mother and father do what they think they have to," she said after a minute. "Nina and I are not in the formula." She let me think about that. "Do you want to come over here right now?" she said.

Vera Ann was typing. She still had deadlines, and the worst of the work for tomorrow was done. Her study door was closed. I left a note saying I would be home soon, love Annie. I was at the little house behind Riva's in seven minutes.

They were both waiting on the porch. Nina held a package wrapped in gold foil. I ran up the walk, but I went slowly up the steps, panting. "We wanted to give you this," Nina said. She smelled earthy, like good clay. "It doesn't matter tomorrow," she said, "whether we're there or not. Right?"

"It matters," I said. "I hate them." I took the package.

"Don't hate them," Riva said.

"Open it now," Nina said.

It was a pendant on a gold chain, a ball smaller than half an inch in diameter, heavy like crystal and filmy and changeful as if it were filled with pale green water.

"I wish I could stay here," I said.

"You could if it were up to us," Nina said.

Riva said, "Some things are important for reasons that seem very strange. It works two ways. Why we're important is strange to your mother, why she's important is strange to you now, when you're eight. But she is. So is this baptism. It needs to please more than just you. Write a poem about it later." But I cried all the way back to my parents' house.

SO YOU CAN SEE THAT RIVA AND NINA RECOGNIZED AS well as I did my true motive for becoming a counselor at Jordan Camp. As usual, they seemed merely to rejoice in my good fortune, the same way they did when I won writing awards and finally a scholarship to a small Eastern university for my poetry. There were blessings and rituals for these occasions, of course, but only rare mention of my parents. If my mother objected to the camping trips we took, the birthday and holiday parties we held over at Nina's, she found subtle ways to say so: *Sundays are for family; you need to be at home for holidays, dear, your father expects it; of course we rejoice in your awards and scholarships, dear, isn't that why we take you to dinner? Good girl.*

When I told her I had applied to be a counselor at the girls' camp, she said, "That will be a pleasant summer job for you." My father said, "Why don't you get a good job writing for IBM?" I believe he regretted having turned down an opportunity in Washington, D.C. His daughter and IBM seemed like a suitable substitute partnership.

CAMP JORDAN IS KNOWN FOR ITS DEMOCRATIC CLIENTELE. Rich little girls' parents pay the full tuition, but less fortunate children are subsidized if their application forms indicate suitable aptitude and desire for "experience in theory and practice of environmental responsibility, astronomical issues and affairs, and physical wellbeing." The camp lies halfway up a ten-thousand-foot mountain raked by ski trails in winter and crisscrossed in summer by family recreational vehicles with license plates from Manitoba to Mexico. We lived just over the mountain from it—ten minutes by small plane, two hours by bus. Sometimes the green camp bus came down into our city for a play or planetarium performance, and I watched the girls with something less than envy. I didn't need to go to camp to love the mountains and the stars, and I hiked everywhere, my essential tools in my backpack, without having to pay any kind of money tuition, full or subsidized.

But once I saw the poster at the community college, that summer before I went away to the East, the image of myself as a counselor fascinated me. I had no idea Riva's daughter would be there.

Of course I had met Riva's children. As I understood it, her husband and she had a congenial arrangement, neither divorce nor cohabitation, once Riva admitted the nature of her relationship to Nina. There were two children, a boy and a girl, very young when this all started, and they lived with their father several miles away. Riva went with them sometimes to family affairs, their own baptisms and priesthood ordinations and family reunions and so on, and sometimes the children came to stay with their mother briefly while their father went on a business trip or somewhere. I learned from Nina to like them, though in a strange, disinterested way, since though I wasn't exactly their rival, I was too old, and too much a part of Riva's life in ways very different from them, to be their friend. Still, they were important to her, and she wouldn't give them up, nor would she let the marriage be dissolved. Riva was, is, Mormon, after all. Husband and children are the crowning glory. I suppose it's to Nina's credit that she accepted all this without complaint.

But the point is that I knew Katie, and Christopher her brother as well. Katie was nine at Camp Jordan, ordinary-looking enough except for those intense brown eyes, young enough to take pleasure in following instructions, being the first to chirp out right answers, making cute new friends. She waved eagerly at me that first afternoon, happy to see a familiar face.

"Annie Macdougal!" she called across the crafts classroom.

"Katie Maynard, as I live and breathe," I called back. "Are you doing your weaving correctly?"

Which, of course, she was. She did everything correctly. Not like her mother in the eyes of the Church; not like me in the eyes of my own mother.

And because she was there, I took her under my wing, as Jesus would have Jerusalem. I made her mine, for Riva's sake. I thought, *now I can pay Riva back.*

WE BEGAN TO DO RITUALS. BUT—LIKE RIVA AND NINA—I did not call them rituals. I called them activities, and we included as many of the other nine-year-old girls as wanted to come. There were always treasure hunts, gifts from the earth. We talked about the elements—the original four, and the chemical hundred and six, and the poetic seven, and the camp three (environmental, astronomical, physical). We starting calling ourselves The Fifth Element. On one trip back to town I even got us T-shirts with our name in neon green. To me, Katie began to look more and more like her mother.

"HAS THERE BEEN A BLESSING?" VERA ANN DEMANDS, SUD-denly here, in the hospital waiting room, a surprise and yet not a surprise. "Why are you sitting here crying? Where is this little girl's father? Should your father come with the bishop? She isn't dead, is she?"

I shake my head. No to everything. Riva should be here, not you, but she is in Canada with Nina at a women's music festival, and I am so afraid.

"I'll go get your father," Vera Ann says. *Her recipe for rightness: go get a father. It's written in all the manuals, how could I have forgotten? She walks away, briskly, her huaraches slapping the linoleum correctly.*

And once she is gone I know what to do.

"KATIE MAYNARD," I WHISPER TO THE CHILD THROUGH the glass. She is in intensive care. A machine is breathing for her. I will not let my brain be filled with the fluid of fear. I put both hands on the glass between us, not caring who's watching, what nurse, what aide, what intern. Glass is only silicon, only sand, and can't stop the healing I send to her. I feel my palms sweating against the double pane, but I also feel them tingling, and I know my mind is set. "Katie Maynard," I whisper. "In the name of our Lord and the Mother I send you the power to be free as air. Warm as fire. Live as earth. One with water. I promise it won't hurt you and you'll know how close you've been. I love you. Your mother loves you. In the name of Jesus, amen."

We've gone around and around about Jesus, Riva and I. But his maleness doesn't bother me at all. I've told her I think the Mormon story is simply not complete, it only knows his air and fire forms though his earth form, his water form, is Mother, and I can pray in the name of Her and to Jesus both and Mormon or pagan or what you will, whatever God is will hear, and Katie will be healed without offense to anyone. So I say this prayer and send the waves of all my health to her through glass, through iron.

"IS THIS THE MAYNARD GIRL?" MY FATHER ASKS THE intern at the door. He nods. My father shows a card. "I'm here to give a blessing." Even the interns here are Mormons and he nods without a shrug. In fact, when he sees there is only my father, not the requisite two priesthood holders, he offers to help. My father accepts. It is what he wanted. My father nods at me as they go in. My hands are still plastered to the glass.

I want to be able to hear, and I can. The intern pours oil on her head and seals her for the blessing. That's in the manuals. That's how they do the blessings for the sick, these men, this lay priesthood of my mother Vera's church. Then my father says the words. I strain to hear. After the ritual invoking of the priesthood and the name of God, he says, "We bless you, Katie Maynard ..." His voice trails off. I know what he has to say next and I wait for him to say it.

"God is with you," he says. "You are not to die. There is something working in you ... the ... elements conspire in your behalf. I bless you to accept them and be whole."

There is a pause. These are words I've never heard my father use before; they're certainly not part of any Mormon blessing. I hold my breath, my hands still plastered to the glass. He finishes with the ritual ending: in the name of Jesus Christ, amen. With his hands still on Katie's head, he opens his eyes and says to the intern, "I have no idea what I meant." They come out of the room after the intern checks her pulse, which is, apparently, all right. My father stares at me as he passes. It's as if he has no idea who I am.

Without Number

1978

MOSES 1:30–33. AND IT CAME TO PASS THAT MOSES CALLED upon God, saying: Tell me, I pray thee, why these things are so, and by what thou madest them? And the Lord God said unto Moses: For mine own purpose have I made these things. … And worlds without number have I created; and I also created them for mine own purpose …

"UP ALREADY?" MY FATHER SAID, HERE EARLY TO FETCH my husband. Developers and investors always on the lookout, they were on their way to Idaho for a site check. Late fall, 1978. "Baby keeping you awake?"

"Haven't been to sleep," I said, rueful. I handed him his morning Postum and he nursed it, letting warmth seep into his big workingman's hands, waiting at the counter for Paul to come downstairs. On B Street in Salt Lake City, November in the Carter years, everything spelled *safety*: well-dusted furniture, vacuumed rugs, lint-free drapes, shining stovetop. Remote threats, distant uncertainties all bided their time. Dad loved Paul the way a father-in-law loves his perfect son-in-law, both of them loved me the way men love their daughter and wife, and there was a baby—Christopher. Another (Katie) was on the way, and I, the best-trained technical writer at Thiokol, knew that I would never want for food, shelter, or community. The minute I wanted to quit working outside the home, I could.

"So what's bothering you?" My father squinted.

I shrugged. "Don't know," I said. "This and that. Little things."

"Problems at work?"

I shook my head, balancing what he would believe against what I wouldn't say. "I don't know what this pattern's about," I said, truthfully enough.

"Sometimes little things add up," he said. "Just don't let it go too far. Hey, Paul." Always the buffer, my husband came to the landing, briefcase in hand, trenchcoat over his arm. Ready to go. Careful and secure.

I'd been out with Paul just twice when my father, his supervisor at Layton Construction, told me confidentially, "Better marry that one. Your mother'd approve. Never seen a better worker." From my father—who raised no hard-driven sons only because his wife died too soon to bear them—there was no higher compliment. Sometimes, during the seventies, I imagined scenarios where my mother bestowed *her* highest compliments —"never heard a funnier storyteller," or "never saw a more talented artist." Well, it was possible. But I didn't check with Dad about this. Enough for him that she'd been a saint, prettiest girl in her class at the U, Lambda Delt pres., stalwart supporter of city and Church. Her death was the tragedy of his life.

And I was the light of it. By the time I graduated from their alma mater with an emphasis in Technical Writing so I'd never be without a job (although secretly I devoured women's lit, so I'd never be without friends)—by the time I graduated, my father, accustomed to Paul's extreme competence, made him head accountant and urged me to join the partnership.

"You let him take you to the temple. He'll take care of you for eternity," Dad said. I was almost twenty-two. Nobody at Thiokol was under thirty-five, and the Mormon engineers were all married with hordes of children. Paul was twenty-four, single, narrow-shouldered and cosmopolitan (from Boise!). He was a prospect, all right. I lay awake at night, tabulating: On the one hand, Paul. On the other—what?

Nobody was surprised at our announcement. Paul accepted the stocks as a wedding gift, but beyond that he said he wouldn't take any more than he earned, so my father had to find ways to give us everything he wanted to. When we burst through the bronzed doors of the Manti temple, my father pulled us aside even before the photographer could snap us kissing in the summer heat.

"Here," he said, cramming the manila envelope into Paul's hands. "Small token of my confidence, son. I know my daughter's never going hungry." Paul was too proud to accept a house or an outright partnership in the company, but too smart not to make sure the stocks rose in value. "You," Dad said, quoting Gordon B. Hinckley, "you *two*, are my most precious assets. Never forget it."

Paul took this as a challenge. Within months we had a mortgage on a house in the Avenues, a historic high-ceilinged brick arrangement on half an acre of sloping lawn and stream, with a handful of fruit trees and a little plot for vegetables. Paul built steppingstones over the creek, a gazebo for shade. Sometimes I strolled out there in the wee hours, wrapped in chenille or silk, counting the stars or the steps. Our neighbors were kind—mostly older, crinkly with pleasure at all that lay ahead for our little family.

"I'm pregnant," I told my father under the autumn leaves one Sunday after dinner. (That was Chris.) Before the weekend, a brand new Voyager sat in the driveway, a bouquet of tiny roses in the front seat. "Car's from me, flowers are from your mother," the card read. Paul bought an infant restraint, even though Utah wouldn't pass the laws for another three or four years. I drove the van seven months before there was anyone to fill it. By day I wrote up specifications for the minutiae of rocketry and ordnance. I was good at detail, careful with punctuation. On my breaks I read fragments of Alice Munro, segments of Ursula LeGuin, snippets of Doris Lessing and Joanna Russ. At the end of the day, dry-throated from hours of peering silently at 10-point typeface, I drove home through mysterious landscape miles and miles in breadth, a bleak marathon of freeway through flat desert, long white lines ahead, in the fall and spring long gray-brown sheets of salt desert to either side, and in the winter, ice, fog-particles, the road mined with hidden hazards like wandering stock or drunk hunters. I feared the sudden appearance of deer. One night at dinner I said so, during a lull.

My father said, "Honey, driving's no different from walking or cooking or breathing. You just do what you have to when the moment comes up, one thing at a time. Pass me that, will you?"

"Hm," I said, passing the salt. "I don't have to deal with big game when I cook." They chuckled. "Walking and breathing don't involve rubber on concrete."

"Asphalt," said Paul, passing the butter.

In the night, I thought *asphalt?*

Christopher was born in April. Thiokol gave me a forward-looking three-month maternity leave. What impressed my father was the request to return, the offer to pay for child care. His daughter must be good at what she did.

"Now, you know your mother took care of you till the day she died," he told me, bobbling the baby in the Land's End chaise longue as Paul mowed the lawn and I harvested early beans. "You really think you need a nanny?"

"Women have always helped each other raise their babies," I said lightly, snapping beans into a bowl. "Help with little things. Just like Mr. Layton has assistants. Vice presidents. Supervisors like you. Same thing." He tried to chuckle.

"If your mother were alive, she'd take the baby for you," Paul said—my father winced—"but she's not. So what *are* you going to do?"

"Good question," Dad said. "What do you want in a nanny? Young and good-looking? Or old and experienced?" He winked at Paul.

"Well read," I said.

Paul grunted. My father said, "I'll have my secretary find some-body to fill the bill," handed me the baby, and headed inside to watch *Mary Tyler Moore*, his favorite. Sometimes, at night, I sat in the La-Z-Boy he'd brought from his house to ours for his after-dinner comfort—I settled into its Naugahyde sags in the night, smelling his cologne, wondering about my mother.

"CHRIS IS TEETHING AGAIN," PAUL SAID ONE MORNING IN October.

"I know," I said, pulling on my Diane von Furstenburg. It wouldn't do for an increasingly-sought-after tech writer to be anything but "chick," said my father. Paul liked to help choose the dresses. This one had a tiny black and white print that could have been letters or puzzle pieces. "Also scooting. Also taking solid foods."

"Nina keeps you informed, then?" he said, referring to the nanny.

"Well, yes," I said, tying the wrap, "but I can see for myself—I feed him dinner. I play with him."

"You're home less and less," he said.

"Look who's talking," I said, trying for a playful tone. "I can't imagine Dad would send you all over the eleven Western states if he were worried about *me*."

"*Somebody* has to be home for the children, one parent pro-viding the head, the other the heart," he said. His tie was smart, a four-inch Italian silk.

I straightened his collar. "What if both parents have heads?"

"Riva," he said. "I want another baby. Children are the jewels in a man's crown. I'm making enough for us to add to our fam-ily without your working." That night as he lay over me I made a claw with my free hand above his back, tense. With the rest of my body I breathed "receptive, open," as I'd learned in birth-ing classes. Afterward I pulled the extra blanket over him and went to sit in the gazebo with my arms crossed over my chest, watching Orion over the mountains through the trees. Let him think I'm willing, I said to myself.

And so I was, because a smooth daily routine mitigates the rougher parts of a marriage. Any wife knows this.

Every weekday for nearly a year, at the end of my drive, Nina was waiting there at home with chili or chops and a perfectly contented child. Like me, she had a degree in something from some university. Unlike me, she didn't use it to make her living; for all I knew, Nina's whole business in life was to come to my house, feed my child, clean my sink, make the meals my husband and I ate together. Having cued me in all my lines concerning the baby's progress, his crawling, his walking, his baby speech, she would slip quietly away, leaving us to our scenario of willing compliance.

Paul and my father and I laughed amiably over supper. Most evenings Paul was in town, we'd wave my father good-bye after *M*A*S*H** or *Rockford Files,* then play with Christopher till he fell asleep. We'd lie on our king-sized waterbed to watch Johnny Carson until after a while Paul reached over absentmindedly and rubbed my feet or other parts, and eventually we ended up asleep tangled around each other. If he was away for the company, doing a site check, settling a stock question, sometimes Nina stayed even after my father left, chatting idly about Christopher, pulling at her long brown braid.

"Do you read?" I asked sometime in January or February. Christopher was hauling himself along the coffee table, precocious. His father was in Arizona.

"All the time," she said. "You?"

When I told her I read fiction on my breaks, she said, grinning, "Sure—to improve your technical style."

"Exactly," I said. "I adapt Munro's techniques—you know, those brilliant character constructions—I connect descriptions of supposedly discrete parts into some visionary whole undreamed of by the engineers."

"I believe you," she said.

"A good tech writer needs acquaintance with multiple worlds." I reached just in time to keep Christopher upright as he came to the end of the sofa.

"You do, that's for sure," she said. "You live on about five different worlds that I can see."

This interested me. "Tell," I said.

"Your dad's a world," she held up her left thumb, which Christopher grabbed. "Your husband." The index finger. "Your work—that's a whole world unto itself." Another finger, pointing at me: "This house. And then there's all that literature you read, all those worlds inside those pages." Christopher swayed, pulling on her splayed hand. "Want to know what I read? Astrology books." She jiggled the baby patiently. "Does that freak you out?"

"Hey, I watch the stars at night," I said. "Now you've made me curious. How many worlds do *you* occupy?"

She stood, scooping up my boy. "Come here," she said, grabbing my hand. We made our way to the gazebo, looked southwest over the city sprawled across the valley. "That's my world—one world, you'd think. Salt Lake City, nineteen-seventy-seven. Unified. Harmonious."

"Uh-huh," I said, rubbing the baby's back, watching the lights.

"But no." I could see her breath. Her eyes—light blue—were bright in the cold.

"No?" I said, shivering just a little.

"Ha!" she said, pointing west toward Temple Square. "There's one—that's your world, too. Six for you, then. I was born into it too. Sure, it's one part of the world that's this city. But I'll bet you don't even know about Cosmic Aeroplane—that's two—or Mormons for ERA—that's three—" My teeth were beginning to chatter. The baby's cheeks reddened in the chill. "Gilgal. That's a whole thing too. Do you know Gilgal? A sphinx with the head of Joseph Smith? Right down there in the middle of town. There are worlds in this town—" Fierce, she was. It surprised me.

"Let's get Christopher inside," I said.

"He'll be okay. I feed him baby vitamins. He won't catch cold."

"I might, though," I said. I pulled her inside, turned up the radiator in the living room, rubbed my hands hard so they'd be warm as I put the baby in his pajamas.

"You might," she said, wry. "I think you're catching something already."

ALL SPRING AND INTO THE SUMMER SHE BROUGHT ASTROL-ogy books from Cosmic Aeroplane, books about light bodies, vibrations in the universe, the flow of the Tao, the paradigm shifts toward which she believed we were irrevocably streaming. She mentioned the ERA, brought newspaper clippings. At the solstice, she lit candles and read from Madame Blavatsky. She believed, with Madame, that everything was a sign. Everything connected at a deep level. We co-create our reality. None of it contradicted anything I already sensed. Politics, esoteric religion, literature: women and men are not what conventional wisdom would have us be, but energy and matter. Consciousness and content. Within this one world lie millions of parallel ones, material or imagined but equally real. We are free agents, choosers, more than we think we are, and different. It all has to do with focus.

When Paul and my father were home, I focused on them.

"They called me to be executive secretary," Paul said one Sunday in September. Tomatoes were on in spades, and once more the leaves were turning. We were eating outside under the sugar maples. Soon there would be frost.

"Of course you said yes." My father cut Christopher's roast into small pieces. "What about you, girl? What's your calling?"

"Mom, I guess," I said. "They haven't called me to anything."

"It's because you work full time," Paul said stiffly. He wiped his mouth hard with his linen napkin. "They told me that this afternoon."

"Well," I said carefully. "That's thoughtful of them, then, isn't it? I don't have time to be a Relief Society counselor."

"You could quit work," my husband said.

"Your mother was stake R.S. pres. when she died, you know," Dad said. Christopher stopped eating. I reached over with my fork, put a bite of tomato in his mouth. He wiggled, happy. "Did I ever tell you about the time the policemen came to tell your mother about the Caribbean cruise I won in that drawing at the firemen's fundraiser? She was having a Relief Society meeting, and when she saw those men in uniform, she grabbed you and hid in the closet. The other sisters had to answer the door. Afterward your mother said all she could think was that they were coming to tell her I'd died and she just couldn't face it. How about that?"

Paul nodded, approving. "Did you ever go on the cruise?"

"No," my father said, sad now. "She was the one who died."

Paul and I didn't say anything.

"You two, you better hang on to each other. That old calling, that's nothing. They're just not inspired to call Riva yet."

"Apparently not," Paul said, pushing back his chair. "However, I'm now the exec sec, and I intend to be fully involved." He snatched up his empty plate.

"That's the way to talk, young man," my father said. He handed Paul his own plate and Christopher's. "Did I hear you say there's strawberries for dessert?" While Paul was inside he scowled at me. "Do I need to be worried about you two?"

"I hope not," I said. "Not unless he's having an affair with Nina or something."

That got a laugh. "Yeah, she's a looker," Dad said. Paul brought the strawberries and we talked about Christopher, business, the yard, till it was too cold to sit outside and we went in the house.

Awake in the night, I tried adding it up: my father's harrumphing loyalty to my mother and the Church; Paul's efforts, his intentions; Joseph Smith's teachings. (Nina took me to the garden of Gilgal, with its strange symbols, and when I took Paul there later, pretending accidental discovery while we walked with Christopher in the stroller, he shook his head, incredulous.) Sonia Johnson's fight with Orrin Hatch. At home, by day, Christopher scrabbled in the yard in miniature corduroys, threw crayons with enthusiasm, lisped, "Mama, Nini, Papa, WANT!" After work I made tomato sauce. Raked leaves. Paul did not have an affair with Nina. That was never my worry.

But then the thing that *was* my worry became a reality: I missed two periods, again. Summer deflated into autumn. The wind blew in a warm winter. No one at Thiokol noticed that sometimes, on my breaks, I cried over the news, over the workload, over my books. What my father noticed was that no matter how early he came to pick up Paul, I was already up. Hadn't slept. Couldn't. And not (though he mustn't know this) because of the baby.

ON THE AFTERNOON OF THE DAY MY FATHER WENT WITH Paul to Idaho, a dark twilight two weeks before Thanksgiving, I made my way to the parking lot, gnawing a cracker, holding off nausea. A storm was coming. The sky bled black behind the plant, an opacity on the horizon west and north, racing me home. I hunched over the steering wheel, tensing myself for the onslaught of that darkness, that hard wall of thunderhead stripping the sky of light. It seemed a sign: I must tell Paul that I was pregnant, tell him and take the consequences. If he and my father said that with two children I must stop working, I would. (Would what? I didn't know.) The wind flung dust and debris against the van, pattering, jittering, setting records a little further north (you can look it up still and find the reports, roofs blown off, damage from limbs and litter). It wasn't rain, but it soon would be. At one point not a deer but a vision of my mother spun out at me from the maelstrom: "Defend her now!" I thought she cried as she flew from her hiding place into the fray.

At home, "Bad night?" said Nina as she took my coat. I shook my hair out, stretching my neck left and then right.

"Pretty bad," I said. "But this place looks great." It always did, clean but not too clean, traces of the baby's dinner in the sink, a skillet of something on the stove. Good jazz on KUER, soft light in the big room holding the wind at bay.

"Both your dad and your husband called," she said, holding the baby out to me.

I raised an eyebrow.

"They won't be back tonight. Your dad's in Ogden. Your husband's still in Poky. He'll call later."

"Okay," I said. Then, "Will you stay?" It came out like that, sudden, unpredictable.

"All night?"

I didn't say no. We bathed Christopher together, laughing at his babbling. I read him *Goodnight Moon* till he dozed on the floor, and then, sleepily, we watched television late into the night, full of comfortable sarcasm at Carson's Carnac silliness. When the phone rang at almost midnight, we both jumped. Nina said, out of a half sleep like mine, splayed as we were across the water-bed, "It's for you," without picking it up.

"I'll be here two nights," Paul said. "Will you be okay? Is there anything I need to know?"

How about you don't come home? I thought. "Everything's fine, take your time," I told him. Christopher stirred at my voice. I got up to rock him. Nina lay back, stretching.

"That baby," she said. "He has a great horoscope, did you know? I drew it up one day when he was sleeping. Moon in his seventh house, Jupiter in his first. Lucky. Just like his mom."

She rolled off the waterbed and took him from me. I watched her dark shape as she left our room, laid Christopher in his bed, and wandered back, graceful, strong, a presence like my mother's, I thought, surely my mother's was a presence like that … She put her hands on my shoulders and kneaded, deep into my neck and up behind my ears. Her hands—I reached up to them, held them. She bent down, kissed my cheek.

"Everything's just fine," she said.

"Is it?" I said.

"Believe it," she said, lifting me by the hand. "Now come on. Come to bed."

"Thank you," I said, and went with her. There was comfort in her arms, and afterward, I slept the rest of the night, oblivious to the hurtling storm, the starless heavy skies to the west, to the north, the cover in all directions black, massive, dangerous.

Pennyroyal, Cohosh, Rue

1980

ABOUT THE TIME I FIRST REALIZED I WAS A FEMINIST I
went to a women's retreat at a little mountain spa an hour's drive
from the perfect home in the Avenues where we were living at
the time. The retreat, one of those such as were advertised in
magazines like *New Age Journal* and the "spirituality" issues of
Ms., attracted about a hundred women willing to dance their
self-portraits, choose new names in a rebirthing ceremony, and
meditate in mooncircles together.

Paul, my husband, wary of this feminist spirituality, said it
was nothing but big business, too much lesbianism, too much
separateness and exclusion. There was evidence in Church history for discussion of a Mother in Heaven, he said, who probably headed the Relief Society or its celestial angel version, but
the private circles, the "rituals" and healings by laying-on of
female hands—those were definitely anti-Church, anti-family,
maybe even anti-Christ. Personally, I thought Christ would be
more open-minded than that. Anyway, I loved them. They were
inward, heart-directed, in contrast (I thought privately) to the
hectic head-centered externalities of my life as a working Mormon mother.

During one of the mooncircles at the retreat, the leaders,
whose names were Roberta and Mary Lou, instructed us to visu-
alize two women we trusted coming to us, dressing us in robes,
and leading us to a sacred space where we were to meet the Goddess, or in other words, our Highest Selves. This exercise was
deeply moving for me, chiefly because of the two women who

came to me. One was my mother, who died when I was very small but who comes to me often in dreams, seeming to love me always, even when I rebel against certain Church policies, even ones I would have thought she held in solemn esteem.

The other woman who came to me in this labor of the imagination was Paul's late Grandma Jean, the most orthodox of her orthodox generation, reputable and honored wife of the patriarch of the Maynard clan. Her coming to me, full of unmistakable warmth and approval, to dress me in full-length Grecian-like robes and then to lead me to a decidedly non-Mormon sanctuary, indicated to me more surely than my mother's appearance that this meditation was not a product of my imagination after all. In my wildest dreams I would not have conjured her up. I suppose I have a right to claim my mother's unconditional love, but Grandma Jean? She was a straight one. She'd not have stood for some of the things I've done. She'd have backed Paul all the way.

Yet during the meditation, she stayed with me, closer and brighter than my mother, and when it was time to return to normal consciousness, it was her embrace that sent me back. I could only sit with my head bowed against my knees, there on the floor of the mountain spa lodge, when Roberta and Mary Lou asked us to share. I couldn't speak.

Grandma Jean had been a beautiful, tall woman, slim-waisted, full-breasted, crowned with white in her last years like a queen. My own grandmother had bowed to osteoporosis (I took megadoses of calcium to prevent the same fate in my own bones) and had died brittle and bent, but Jean stood straight and met your eye fully, even when she was eighty-four and hadn't long to live. She was a gifted storyteller, much in demand at socials, holding adults and children alike in thrall repeating "The Cask of Amontillado" from memory, or "A Child's Christmas in Wales," or the story of Joseph and the coat of many colors, somehow making connections between that Joseph and Joseph Smith in the grove at Palmyra.

Her grandchildren were also treated to other stories, personal rather than community ones. Paul, and his sister Suzanne, too, told me these accounts were entertainment of the highest order, pass-alongs, myths to live by for the Maynard youth, who were convinced once and for all that they could never live up to her standards. Our generation was hopeless. All the adventures, all the trials and consequences in the universe, had already been suffered by Paul's parents and numerous uncles and aunts, and even, in one or two cases, by Jean's very own friends.

One of these stories I was fortunate to hear in person, one afternoon early in my courtship with Paul, when I was still a trophy to show off to all the family's women (Grandma Jean, Paul's older sisters, and their own blossoming daughters). Grandma's storytelling, and this story in particular, fit a certain startling pattern just beginning then to take a shape inside the edges of my awareness. No wonder Grandma Jean came to me during that retreat. I see that now. No wonder I couldn't speak after.

GRANDMA JEAN WAS THE CHILD OF A POLYGAMIST. HER youth was full of children and "aunts."

"But," she told me that afternoon in the spring of 1975, "we were rich. We weren't like some of those fundamentalists you see around today, dozens of children and no income, just rags and hungry eyes. Land, no. Eighteen of us lived in the same house, but it had ten bedrooms and two parlors, up there in Morgan, and our mothers got along wonderfully well. They were smart. They worked it so we didn't have to hide. You know this was after even the second Manifesto against polygamy in 1904. But they were careful and called each other 'sister,' and our dad kept up the farm and kept us in shoes every winter and we were peaceful. Luckier than a lot of folks."

Luckier especially than the Caldwells. Grandma's best friend in those days was Beleatha Caldwell, third child of the first wife of Heber. They were both ten years old when Brother Caldwell married two young sisters on the same day, just a month after

Beleatha's mother died, leaving seven children. Both of these new wives were fertile as rabbits, Grandma Jean said, conjuring up in my mind images of fluffy children hopping around a grassy side-yard, chewing lettuce and carrots. In five years there were seven more Caldwells. Beleatha and Jean used to sit on the fence bordering Brother Caldwell's pasture and giggle about the diapers draped everywhere to dry. When the older of the two new wives died in the smallpox outbreak of 1908, the other, Prudence, with Caldwell Number Fifteen "in the oven," as Grandma put it, took on primary responsibility for them all, and then for the farm as well when Brother Caldwell was called on a mission to England. Jean saw Beleatha less and less as she was needed more and more to watch the little ones and help with meals and housework, though she still got away from time to time and giggled as much as ever when she did.

Until the time Jean went over just in time to see Beleatha trying to hold Prudence back while Prudence slashed at some chickens in the yard, chopping right and left with the old axe, feathers and blood everywhere and horrible squawking, not just from the chickens but from Prudence too. This was no ordinary butchering, Grandma said; there was something disorderly about it, frightening and wasteful, and she never could bring herself to mention it to Beleatha, but ran home quickly before she was seen.

This was not long after Michael Adam, the baby, was born. Subsequently, Grandma said, Beleatha did not come out any more to giggle by the fence. And the Caldwell children began to look increasingly ragged and strange.

One day, Peggy May, the nine-year-old, came to school in one of Prudence's temple garments with its sleeves and legging parts rolled up and pinned back, supposedly so she could move and cipher properly. The teacher hustled her over to Sister Carpenter's in a twinkling, and they put something else on her, but nobody had missed the long white underwear dangling on

Peggy's frame. Another day, Sam, who was two, was seen toddling across the canal bridge, trailing his diapers and bawling for all he was worth. Sister Rosas brought him home to her house and kept him for a week.

The oldest Caldwell boy, Matt, had a hard time keeping up with the farm. Naturally most of the men tried to come lend a hand, and the next brother, William, did the best he could to help, but during the summer harvest Prudence got on the buckboard and flogged one of the horses to death. Then she left it lying in the middle of the field and took herself into the house to bed. It was difficult for anybody to know what to do after that. Nobody wanted his own horses overworked, and the family seemed less and less inclined to accept help anyway.

"'Pathetic' was a soft word for it," Grandma Jean said briskly. "The bishop refused to send for Brother Caldwell off his mission. Of course it would have taken months to get the word to him and get him home anyway, but he should have been told what was happening to his wife and household. Beleatha looked grimmer and grimmer. So'd the whole lot of 'em—grim and ragged. It was obvious to everyone that Prudence was losing her mind."

The day Prudence shot the babies it was summer's end. Most ladies were home canning tomatoes and pickles, checking melons for ripeness, sending the children off to play at the canal under the watchful eye of Missy Praetor, who'd been to the coast and knew how to swim well enough to save lives if need be. William Caldwell had brought in a load of hay the day before and figured he deserved a break, so he was down at the canal making eyes at Missy. Beleatha had come away too. She and Jean were picking the blackberries that bore like crazy along the pasture fences.

"Things seemed gratefully calm for the moment," Grandma said. "All afternoon I'd seen the Caldwell kids coming in and out of the house, some with what I thought were bundles of wash, one or two with boxes. Then I heard a low unusual sound, like an animal moaning. Prudence came to the door with the baby hanging over one arm and one of her sister's children hanging over the other. Remember, Prudence couldn't have been more than twenty-four, and that baby—the youngest of fifteen, ten of whom were under nine—was about three months old. He'd been colicky, poor thing. Even the midwife's peppermint tinctures didn't help his screaming.

"Prudence came to the door like that and Beleatha said, 'Oh-oh, she's going to want me now,' and started picking up her buckets and getting ready to go in. But it was the oddest thing. Prudence just stood there in the doorway. Not calling. Not anything. She looked left and right, like she didn't even notice us, and then she turned around and staggered back inside and shut the door. Beleatha and I remarked how quiet it suddenly seemed. No children crying. No dogs barking. I remember Beleatha cocked her head with a puzzled frown at the exact moment two shots were fired from inside the house.

"Beleatha was out of those berry bushes in two leaps—I tore after her through the weedy garden and across the doorstep in less time than it takes to tell—the door was barricaded—we pounded on the west window till it fell open and I pushed Beleatha up through it. I can still see her patched underwear like it was yesterday. And when I scrambled up after her and got inside, I wished I hadn't, because there in a puddle of blood lay the baby Michael Adam, and the other baby—I think its name was Jennifer—sat staring in a corner, mouth open, without a breath, without a sound.

"Prudence held the gun to her chest like a cross. The children were dead. Beleatha screamed—I thought she'd never quit. William came, and he went and got some of the men, and they took Prudence and those two pathetic bodies, in the most shocked and slow and silent afternoon I've ever witnessed. I'd crossed a threshold. You think nothing can shake you again so deep, after such unthinkable business.

"After that, women started to come into the house, one every day, leaving their own families as if they didn't have enough to do, and the children got fed and taken care of, and eventually Beleatha more or less became the mother, although she never had to do it all alone. The Relief Society saw to that. Brother Caldwell came home many weeks later, but I never forgave him for not coming home in time to stop the carnage before it ever happened."

"Why did Prudence do it?" one of Paul's little nieces asked.

If Grandma Jean had been a lesser woman, she might have shrugged, might have advised the girl to come to her own conclusions. But she was regal—a Maynard—and she gave it to her straight: "Well, child, some said it was the heat. Land, it *was* a hot summer. And some blamed the bishop, too, for sending off Heber Caldwell in the first place.

"But I know another thing or two.

"Beleatha told me Prudence aspired to be a midwife—noble work then and now, more trusted by most women than men doctors any time. She told Beleatha that if she could know what midwives knew, she could handle any situation that came up. And the way Beleatha said 'situation,' I knew Prudence meant things I was supposedly too young to have wind of. What I think was, Prudence just got trapped. She saw herself backed into a corner too tight and too deep ever to come whole out of, all her life drifting away in diapers and dust. That's what those bundles were that the little Caldwells were taking out of the house before—Prudence sent them down to the canal with clean diapers and baby clothes and told them to throw them in. That was how William knew something was wrong. He was halfway home when he heard the shots."

"She did it because she was right crazy," said the girl's mother, Paul's sister, Suze.

"Post-partum psychosis," I said.

Grandma Jean nodded. "I still think it was Caldwell should have been shot, and Prudence brought back to normal life with the gentlest of care."

"What happened to Beleatha?" I asked.

"Oh, she became a midwife," Paul's grandmother said, but her attention was wavering. Grandma Jean involved herself totally when she was in the midst of a story, but once it was over, it was over. She had other things to think about. It was only later and quite by accident that I heard any more about Beleatha Caldwell.

ON A SATURDAY A FEW MONTHS AFTER THE RETREAT, MY by-then husband and Suze and I were preparing potatoes to bake for a Maynard family gathering. Paul and I attended these parties regularly, a kind of concession between us to my growing convictions about women holding the priesthood, abortion rights, and certain other issues. Paul needed his family's traditions and rituals to stay in place, and I could certainly sympathize with that. Suze liked to listen to me talk even though she didn't feel the same way I did and said she preferred to retain her temple recommend (though I hadn't lost mine yet). Paul's brother, Ron, never took me seriously anyway and talked to me mainly about the quality of my three-bean salad, which had always been excellent. The rest of the Maynards were the same, keeping to safe topics, but they gave my children water balloons along with everybody else's and we all spit watermelon seeds together in the traditional yearly contest, so there were never hard feelings and in fact I actually enjoyed the reunions very much.

As we washed the potatoes this time, then, the topic of conversation rolled around to Eliza, Paul's cousin's teen-aged daughter, who had just miscarried a fetus conceived out of wedlock.

"What excellent fortune," I said.

"Her mother's brokenhearted," Paul said, disapproving.

"Why? It wasn't her baby," I said.

"It would have been if it had been born," Suze said.

"Did she want that?" I asked. "I wouldn't."

"You'd reject your own grandchild?" my husband said.

"Well, I wouldn't want to raise it," I said. "I'll have had enough raising my own children. I don't need to raise another generation."

He made an exasperated noise. He was always exasperated in those days—but then, so was I.

"Would you raise it?" Suze asked Paul, curiously.

"I wouldn't have to," he said, and then he realized what he'd said and grabbed another potato and scrubbed relentlessly.

Suze and I exchanged a look. There was puzzlement in her eyes.

"What *now*?" Paul was gruff.

"Oh, silly me." Suze swiped at her face with the heel of her hand. "Just thinking about Grandma."

"What about her? You know she was ready to go. It was probably a relief to Ron and his wife when the end finally came." Paul scrubbed away.

"Right. Here." Suze handed Paul another bowl full of potatoes. "Slash these for the oven, will you?"

Then she spoke aside to me. "You know, I have a feeling about you and Grandma Jean. I found something among her papers you might be right interested in. I'll give them to you later. I can't—" seeing Ron approach, the patriarch now of his siblings' families as well as of his own—"I won't say any more now."

Later, diverting Paul's attention from anything wayward, she handed me two big manila envelopes, saying they were full of diaries and other personals and I'd probably be the best one to go through them. "You'll know why when you read 'em," she told me. "Let me know if it's everything I think it is, will you?"

The children fell asleep in the back of the minivan on the way home, so I pulled out the envelopes as Paul drove. There were several small plastic bags with what looked like a layer of dirt in them, and several ruled pages, torn as if from a ledger, covered with Grandma Jean's even, upright handwriting. She had taught Paul, whose handwriting was also even and upright, and who never ceased to be dismayed at my own loopy scrawl.

There was little of interest to me or to anyone else in these pages, I thought at first. They were dated during several weeks in a spring of the Depression, years before Paul was born. Everyone knew how Grandma Jean had struggled to go to nursing school during those pre-war years and had earned her LPN certificate. It was this training, I thought, that had made her meticulous in matters of hygiene and female rhythms. Everyone also knew that Grandpa had been promoted to a lucrative (for those days) traveling job shortly after she got her license, so that Grandma Jean had elected to stay home and be a live-in parent instead of a working one. She was proud of this choice, proud of the "jewels" that were her children, proud of the ways she'd put her skills and talents to work at home and in the Church. Paul had been raised not only listening to his grandma's stories, but also eating her homemade bread, sleeping under her hand-tied quilts, and playing with her plaster-headed dolls, hand-molded and hand-painted. In the family she was held up as womanhood perfected—domestic, creative, organized, content. Paul hinted from the first that few could live up to her example.

I read through the ledger pages for twenty or thirty miles, lulled almost to sleep myself by entries full of people to visit, dinners to arrange, meetings to attend, funerals to oversee. Then, on a Thursday in 1938, this notation:

Day 30. Beleatha Caldwell and an Ogden address.

I read on.

Friday. Day 31. Beleatha says: 2X pennyroyal. X cohosh. X rue. 3x/day. Tea tastes vile, but I'll keep taking it.

Day 33. No one must know. I take the tea quickly when no one can see. What would bishop say? Maynard must have no inkling!

Day 39. Hateful today, worst ever. Screamed at poor Eva and the littler ones. This = female? Hope to know soon. Eva, Paul and Suze's mother, would have been seventeen. There were five younger siblings.

Day 40. Blood! Thank God. I'll keep the tea against a next time, God forbid.

I folded the papers back into their creases and tucked them deep in my bag, under the baby's diapers.

"Anything interesting?" Paul asked.

"A recipe," I said. "That's about all."

A few days after that, I made a few phone calls that confirmed my suspicions. Then I called Suzanne.

"It's what you thought," I said.

"Take care of those papers, will you? Burn 'em?"

"Burn them? I don't think so," I said.

Ron need never know, the bishop will never hear. I'm sure Grandpa Maynard, who died before Paul was even born, never had a clue. But believe me, Suze, I'll take care of them. I'll keep them for our daughters, all sisters of the circle whose membership I less and less deny. The courage of our mothers—the grace of the Goddess to those who say no for their own good and the glory of Her Who is One-in-Herself—these things will not be forgotten.

Cat Woman

1990

IT'S CHRISTMAS, OR WILL BE NEXT WEEK, BUT I, ADELA Suaros, math teacher at The Waterford School and secretary of the Relief Society of the Hillside Stake, Salt Lake City, have resented the season for years now. Resentment is useless, my rebel colleague Riva tells me as we daydream other jobs, other locations, and she half makes me laugh at my own complaints. But only half. This winter is bitterly cold already and gray, dull-metal silver with the polluted inversion that plagues this valley in December and January so that light is dim and breathing measurably difficult. Logan, our two-year-old, suffers from asthma, and already my husband Carlos and I are spending nights holding him upright after he's been dosed with his prescriptions just so he can breathe. It's the worst part of winter, come earlier than usual this season, and it offends me. I'm a stickler for fairness. I don't appreciate my family's exclusion from health and peace by such ephemera as light or breath, or lack thereof. So when the alarm rings at 6:00 a.m., and NPR pumps out some esoteric harpsichord, I pull up my mother's star quilt, hunkered in bed, curled up and blank to the hard weather. "Couperin's *Barricades Mysterieuses*," they announce cheerfully. "Winter storm warning for tonight. Stay home if you can!"

I'd like to pretend I don't have to get Logan up and ready for daycare as usual, don't have to be in a high school computer classroom, calm and detached, at eight to once again monitor honors students, integrating cutting-edge technology and math education in a postmodern, rational way.

Of course, I do get up. But I'm bothered.

"Something happened yesterday," I tell Carlos in the shower. He's scrubbing my back. It's a good time to confess. I tell him about the face I saw in the monitor yesterday when Peter Hollister raised his hand for help. Peter wants to know everything. He always needs help.

"I tried to log on, and nothing happened, Mrs. S.," he said. I typed in the generic login and password and saw on the screen a snarling face, real as a video clip, seeing me, her eyes—definitely a woman's eyes—meeting mine, her dirty, nail-bitten hands clenched close to her terrible bared teeth.

Peter said, "Thanks, Mrs. S.!" He clicked on a link and went right to work. Saved by a password. He didn't seem to have seen what I saw.

"Thought you saw," my good husband says. He turns me to face him so he can soap my breasts. "You're hallucinating. Too many nights up with Logan. Or"—this is why I love Carlos, his lawyer instincts advocating for me—"what was it?"

There it is again, the snarling face in front of my eyes. I lean against the wall of the shower, my eyes closed. "I am exhausted," I admit. "Log's meds don't work." I'm thinking. Grudgingly. "Doc said give it 72 hours to kick in, but four days? Don't they know anything about pediatric asthma?"

The loofah on my arms and neck comforts, the warm water hypnotizes me kindly. But no. Right now, perplexity before pleasure. I say, "Something was going on with that computer." I'm no expert in computers. This job is a stopgap, a step to the rest of my life, the true nature of which I don't know yet, though Riva is helping me find clues through our winter-weary talks. But the face in the monitor was not about fatigue.

"Want me to give Log a blessing?"

A blessing? I shake my wet head to clear it. "You think that would help?" Carlos knows I doubt. Among many other things, on occasion I doubt I'd have chosen this religion he and I were both born into. I'm not into mysteries. But Mormonism is, I've pointed out repeatedly, not only one of the largest and fastest-growing Christian sects in America, maybe the world, but also a mystery cult. Witness the book from the bowels of a mountain, the visionary teenaged prophet, the temples where the faithful do work for the dead—new names, cleansings, redemption. Blessings! He's a high councilor, we're both active members. But it's all mystery.

I push away Carlos's hands, now teasing my nether regions. Fine hands. Blessing hands. Like all good Mormon parents, his taught him to take them for granted—blessings and mysteries.

Evalina, his mother, does genealogy these days as if there were some virtue in it that would keep her alive forever. Stereotypically spry, still shoveling her own walks in the winter, golfing in the summer, she's gone to Brazil or Portugal to look at gravestones every autumn for the past ten years. As she was doing the temple ceremony in proxy for one of her own dead ancestors, long-ago Europeans whose sturdy (if asthmatic) classical genes my boy carries, she says she nearly fell asleep at one point when she felt a tap on her shoulder. She looked around, and no one was there.

Well, it could have been one of the helpers. That's what they're supposed to do, help you through—remind you of the words you forget. But she says it happened again. Every time she nodded off, every time she looked, no one was there. Maybe it's inevitable that if you're standing in for a dead person, you expect strange happenings, unexplainable details. Mysteries. But right here, right now—blessings? Faces in the computer? "I can't think about it," I say, pushing out of the shower. "Really, hon." But before I can grab the towel, Carlos's hand rests on the small of my back. He is rarely in the kind of hurry I always am.

"Tell me about the computer thing," he says, pulling my head to his chest. "Mom says nothing's so important a little attention can't help."

I yield. "She's right," I say into his collarbone. She's one of the wise ones. "But just for a minute."

"Sure," he says, climbing out of the shower after me. He knows I have to get to work. He wraps the bath sheet around both of us, sheltering. "Tell me." And the furious face from the computer appears. I know—how do I know this?—she hates everybody. Including me.

Including Carlos. Thoroughly.

"Whoa," I say.

"Push through," he says.

"I can't stop it anyway," I say. I describe it as it happens. The woman's story comes at me in a series of insistent images, the background sound of the shower still running a soft white noise in my awareness, Carlos's arms around me a soothing presence. Now the snarling face is covered with knotted hair. Now it bends downward, the hands, with extraordinarily long fingernails, covering it. The entire image seems vivid red, as if backlit by a violent video game. I'm meant to make something of this, I know. I have to pay attention.

Carlos holds me while the story plays out like some kind of video cartoon, except that it's a real, eighteenth-century European woman in there, not a jerky-limbed android hybrid. First a little girl runs wild, screaming. Her life is bound up with the lives of women, caregivers who suffer her. That's the word that flashes almost subliminally, like the two-second instructional banners at the bottom of my students' work screens. Only theirs have never said this: *suffer*. This child suffers, and is suffered to remain.

An older woman with a gray braid and a stout, coarsely bloused bosom feeds the child and holds her, much more kindly than any cartoon I've seen in the last five years. Another (the older woman's daughter? The wild child's sister?) stays just out of reach of the child's screaming, scratching fingernails. Now (a flash of graphics), she is a young woman on the edge. I understand this word "edge" to be both literal and metaphorical, both emotional and physical. She stands, hissing, just outside a group of young women who should have been her peers. Something is seriously wrong with her, has been wrong from the beginning. She can't speak. She only spits and shrieks. But the old woman and her daughter have suffered her to live, have made sure she stays alive, clean and fed, though she pushes at them always and sometimes rakes their skin.

The others in the village call her "cat woman." But it's pre-superhero, pre–Michelle Pfeiffer. I hear nothing—what comes at me is all visual—but I can see her hiss and scratch, and she knots her own hair with clawing fingers. I know she dies like that. She never gets better.

"I'm so sorry," I mumble into Carlos's chest.

"For what?" he asks.

"All her life," I say, in a sort of trance, "she's watched those other young women marry, have children, live smooth unbroken lives. Her brain's so jagged … she can't—oh, wait."

Unbelievably (another flash of color), and only by the grace of her caretakers, she grows to old age, sitting in corners, taken care of by other women, the daughters and granddaughters of her original woman-family. These other women she treats miserably. At her death—I realize I know—many of them are relieved. She's been a burden to them, even if they haven't had to wash and feed her. They've seen her and said to themselves, "We could have been like her."

She's known this, too, only in converse terms. All she ever desired in all her life was to be like them. Normal. Womanly. Able to speak what she feels, able to function properly, all parts of her body, all parts of her brain. But the secret key was lost. What she wanted could never be hers.

Finally I know she's died, unhealed, unloving, unfulfilled. I'm there. It may be a dream, but I am connected somehow to this visual across time and space, and I'm tense with sorrow and anger. What would Riva say?

SUDDENLY CARLOS IS MOVING AWAY FROM ME, STANDING me upright, gathering his robe around himself, urgent, insistent. "Listen! It's Logan—you'd better wake up. Hurry!" He throws me a wrap. Together we follow the sounds of the wheezing, dash to the room where Logan is coughing, barely getting in enough air to make the next outbreath, panicked, jerking, unable to make a sound. We throw on sweats and jackets, bundle him in his coverlet, and run.

In the next four hours, we will spin over frozen streets to the hospital emergency room. I will ask Riva to take my place at school, I will loudly denounce the doctor whose prescriptions have been so ineffective. Carlos will call Evalina for support, catching her at home just before she leaves to go to her near-daily session at the temple. Her second home.

"Do you think I can do anything right there, right now? I'm just on my way to do initiatories for this new name I found on the last trip to Lisbon. My namesake! An Evalina! What if I come as soon as I'm done? Barely an hour, and I'll be there."

I protest, but Carlos suggests that she's right, there's probably little she could do here immediately. She might as well enact the rites she loves, praying for her grandson as she stands in for her great-great-great-ancestress So we pour the meager efforts of our hearts over our little boy as he pants more and then less convulsively, clings to our hands, scratching in terror if we let go for a moment. Doctors come, observe, administer, depart. At one point, Carlos puts his hands on Logan's head and murmurs ritual words. I wish for Riva, who knows herbs and does healings, but she is standing in for me at the school, and Carlos is strong and true. I trust his faith as far as I can. Logan is quiet for the blessing and wheezes less fearsomely afterward.

When Evalina arrives, she holds us all in her embrace. "I put his name on the prayer roll," she assures us. "I did the work for, let's see … Evalina Serena Silvestre, 1742, from a mountain village in Brazil called São Sacramento. And you know? I felt peaceful. He'll be all right."

Shortly after, nurses inject our boy with something that finally quiets his attack. We get a new prescription, which maybe this time will work. Logan says, wanly, "Mommy—home?" and that's where we all go.

Now it is snowing hard. Such weather often pushes out the inversion, and though visibility is poor to drive, I'm glad of the snow, the veil of white fanning away the infernal gloom. At home, I hold Logan in the rocker by the window. Carlos turns the humidifier's spray toward us as we look out into the snow. Briefly, so that I almost don't see it, a clear, untwisted face appears in the window, a hand raises. I am almost sure I see it, the fingernails on the hands cut, the hair smooth. *Release* flashes behind my eyes—not an instruction but a report—and *grateful.* Breathing slow and deep, as if I could inspire my boy's lungs to work properly on their own, I rub his back. Carlos puts one hand on top of mine, with the other offers Logan something warm to drink from the kitchen. "Sank you, Daddy," our little boy says, and sleeps within minutes. I'm faint with gratitude. Help from anywhere, I'm thankful.

Shortly after, we tuck Logan back into bed, his head propped up on two pillows. Hand in hand, we return to the living room to send Evalina home. I try to tell her about the cat woman and about what I saw just now, in the storm. I know I sound inarticulate and exhausted. "Ah," she says, nodding. Smiling. "Goodness works in many worlds. I'm glad the child is well."

When she has left, we head back to our own room and lie close to each other, warming ourselves under the star quilt, luxuriating in the possibility of a few hours' rest. "Mysterious," he says once. We lie quietly for a time. Then we turn toward each other, letting things work themselves out through the skin and tongue, wordless, unexplainable, all puzzlement and love.

Pigs When They Straddle the Air

1995

THE REAR OF THE CHEVY DRAGGED DANGEROUSLY. NEARLY twenty years of marriage packed tight in paper and peanuts scraped across the dips between access and freeway, thudded over the curb when Suzanne stopped for gas. Three or four hours into the drive she felt them pulling her backwards, down the west slope of the Sierra foothills, resisting the upward tilt. She kept driving, though, putting the valley behind her whether she wanted to or not. By the time she stopped at the small mountain resort which was her destination for the evening, half the boxes and the flower press had piled against the back window, so that she couldn't see anything in her rear view mirror except cardboard planes and angles. This was how she came to smash the front bumper and right headlight of the motor home parked in the space behind her. She backed in so she could drive out facing forward in the morning, but she misjudged the distance to the Winnebago's high flat front, and she heard glass breaking and felt the car grind to a stop before she put her foot all the way down on the brake.

"I never had an accident before," she told the gentleman behind the counter, who looked like a Middle Easterner in a turban, showing his white teeth the way they do, all unaware of the trouble she'd caused in the lot out front. "I just rammed somebody's big RV." He stopped smiling.

A bristly-jawed young man slouching against the wall cranked his head around, jerking a greasy lock out of half-open eyes. "Big RV?" She could smell the pot, or whatever it was, as soon as he opened his mouth, even from five feet away. "Any identifying marks?" he said.

"A fish bumper sticker and an Arizona plate, but they're crumpled now. It's right unfortunate." Suzanne was prepared to apologize. This was a bad blunder, but she meant to make it right.

"Hey, Dad," said the boy. "Lady here hit our wheels." From a corner table rose a man with a chest tight in a triple-extra-large Pendleton and hands like saddlebags.

"Hell!" the man said. "You smashed the 'bago?"

"Made an effin' concertina outa the front end. You still praisin' the Lord?"

Suzanne's ears perked up. "Concertina"? But then she winced at those other hacked-off words, that bad language. Phil used to report that at the college they were saying things like "all speech patterns and all behaviors are to be respected," but she wouldn't have predicted such a combination of high and low. High and low what? How? She surprised herself by wanting to figure it out. Wasn't that some kind of respecting?

The big man laid one hand carefully on the table and used it as a fulcrum to lever himself toward the counter. "You believe in Jesus?" he asked Suzanne, probably to divert her from his lurching, which she doubted was a physical disability. Whether or not she believed in Jesus was none of his business. Before she could say yes, he hiccupped. "The Lord will provide!" He grabbed at the counter to steady himself.

"My insurance will provide," she said. "Here's the card."

"Praise the Lord. Are you saved?" The hairs in his ears were gray, but his moustache and beard were red. So were his eyes.

"I think I'll make it to Reno, thank you," she told him. "Why don't you let me take your name so we can get this problem taken care of?" She and Phil had always made sure things were taken care of. Insurance, annuities, things like that. That was why she could just shut the door on the house and come away. Good planning, good records, righteous goals—these things gave you freedom.

"There won't be a problem," the son said. He watched Suzanne like a dog on point, and he never blinked. Suzanne's eyes watered when she noticed it. "This here's my dad, Savin' Sam Finn. He can heal your ills and make the whole goddam world a place you love to be. Can't you, Daddy-o?"

"We got the truth, all right," Savin' Sam said. "Me and Sean, here, we got the truth sewed up."

"Well, I feel bad about your vehicle." Suzanne thrust her hands in the pockets of her jacket, a nice blue boiled wool Phil had bought for her last Christmas—if only they'd known it was the last Christmas!—a jacket just right for the Bay Area, but maybe not quite warm enough for the mountains, these or the ones she was headed for—Salt Lake City, that was—now, on an early May evening. She hunched her shoulders. "Shall we go out and have a look at the damage?"

"That 'bago's carried us miles for the Lord," Sam said. "We've seen trials to grieve Jehovah himself. If we just pretend this didn't never happen, will you look up the Jesus Loves You Chapel in Sparks and make a donation? It's clear you're a prayin' woman. Your dollars'll satisfy my needs. What do you say?"

"I don't plan to stop in Sparks," Suzanne said. "I'm going straight through to my brother in Salt Lake, him and his children. I mean to press the spring blossoms with my niece like I always do. Poor girl's got no mother, you see."

"Hey," said Savin' Sam. "Neither's m' boy."

Before he could go off on a distraction, she hurried to say, "The presses got in the way, which is why I crunched your motor home, but it was certainly not intentional. Take the card, please. My insurance—"

Sean Finn reached with the hand not employed by the cigarette and laid it on Suzanne's extended wrist. His fingers were cold. "Chill, old lady. You don't have to worry 'bout a thing." His dirty nails were yellow around the edges like a burnt page, but maybe that was just the fading light. Involuntarily, she pulled her arm away. The card skidded across the floor and into the tiny space between the concierge's desk and the hardwood floor.

"Oho," the boy said. "She don't want grace, Daddy."

"Well, now, that's hard to believe," said Savin' Sam. "Surely that ain't true. This boy here, you know he's in a state of grace. His poor mother left this earth the day he left her womb, and all his trials stem from that. I've done all I can to see the Lord pours down his blessings on every day of his life, but you know he don't take kindly to rejection."

"I'm not rejecting anybody," Suzanne said firmly. She plucked the card from the Middle Eastern fellow. He'd bent courteously to pick it up, dusted it off, and let it go across the counter with a bow. "Your hands are dirty, that's all."

"So are yours now," Sean said, accurately enough. "Pride goeth before a fall."

"It do. It do." Savin' Sam scraped one arm across his own nose, leaning on the elbow of the other. "He smells, don't he?" He put it so conversationally that Suzanne was half-drawn in, almost answered "yes," as if they were new acquaintances sharing observations. She stopped herself in time though. He went on, "It's too bad. I can't control his every move. A life in a RV ain't as easy as some I can think of. In a RV you can't let little things bother you. I'm sorry to see you do." He reached for the card, missed it, reached again. When Suzanne placed the card firmly in his palm, he stuffed it in his shirt pocket and took his son by the arm. "Come on, boy."

His son yanked his arm from his grasp, but together they turned their backs to her and pushed through those big carved doors surrounded by—what were they, elk horns? What was that supposed to mean, elk horns all around the door? She followed them out into the dusk. Before she could decide the appropriate thing to say next, they both climbed into the Winnebago, one on either side of the damaged cab, and clanked the creaky doors shut, one-two. She watched them back the machine out, its one headlight dim in sympathy with its broken partner. The wheels seemed to wobble as they made their way onto the highway.

"That man should not be driving," she said to the registrar, who'd followed her out.

"No, ma'am," he said with a bow. "May I take your luggage to your room?"

BEFORE NINE IN THE MORNING—NOT AN EASY NIGHT, BUT she'd managed to avoid negative thoughts about the previous day's events by reading scriptures and writing in her journal till she fell asleep—by eight-forty-eight, she was on her way east again. The summit was an hour away, and she drove slowly, looking for flowers. She stopped to inspect a stand of buttercups in a small valley, but they were too dewy to press. Waiting for the sun to burn the dampness off, she sat on the back gate of the Chevy and picked up a random album, one of twenty or so six-inch-thick collections of heavy press blotters, big ones in whose margins Phil used to write poems with inks that matched the blooms. No matter how banal the sense of his poems, they were still his. She hadn't let anyone read them aloud at his funeral, but that didn't mean she was ashamed, just that she knew their relative worth, which was that he enjoyed the exercise of writing them. Rhymes made him happy. He'd been a good husband, a good father; if she could wish he'd been a little more educated, a little more classy, well, that was all water under the bridge now that he was gone, wasn't it? The funeral had been decorous, the little funeral home full, and then Phil was laid to rest on Mount Tam, really such a pretty cemetery, and Suzanne had shaken hands with the men and hugged the women and then gone home, packed up what she wanted in the big Chevy wagon, locked up the house and driven away. She'd been fifteen years in San Rafael. It was time to go home to Utah.

A shadow smoking a cigarette chilled her hand on the album page, and a foot in a frayed rope sandal stepped up on the back gate beside her. "Well," Sean Finn said. "Small world, isn't it?"

Suzanne clapped the book shut to hide her startlement. "What are you doing here?"

He gestured, as to the whole wide world. "My father decided he could do with some different company and let me out pretty quick last night. I slept right over there. See?" He pointed to a depression in the grass.

"He let you out? Wasn't it cold?" She couldn't see a blanket.

"Mind if I sit?" She did, but he made himself to home. The tailgate bounced under his added weight—which wasn't all that much, but still. "Actually, me sleepin' out is an old routine. Butterfly Ranch is right over this hill, see, we're in Nevada over there, you know, and when some little caterpillar catches Daddy's eye, he wants to hop into the cocoon and metamorphose, you know? And he lets me out, and I catch up later. A cycle we perform regularly."

Suzanne was not shocked—she was a little old for that, and she knew what the world was like—but she did not approve, either. "Well, I'm sorry to hear that," she said. The boy—what was he, seventeen? He might have been handsome if he groomed himself, shaved, didn't smoke. Really, Suzanne was glad—not for the first time—that her daughters all planned to marry good men and live their lives in the land of Zion, where hopefully they would *not* abandon (or be abandoned by) their families, unlike this boy's father, or, to be honest, that tragic ex-wife of Paul's. She made a little "tch" with her tongue.

Almost as if in response, the boy farted loudly and grinned.

She shook her head. "Expressive, aren't you?"

The grin gave way to shame, or maybe self-satisfaction. She gave him the benefit of the doubt. "'Scuse *me,*" he said. "I should know better. 'Specially in front of an old lady."

At that she sat up straight. Not so old. Forty. And she was smart—she had a bachelor's degree in Family Science from BYU, circa 1976—and she hadn't lost her looks, at least not yet. "Watch your language," she said.

"I always do," he said. "I'm a poet. I turn the words of truth to dust and dust to words of truth," he said—no, *declaimed*. "My father is lower than dust: The words he speaks twist and turn beneath my feet like worms. Loathing flows between us like a cataract of fire. I stay with him for my blessed mother's sake, but the moment he's dead, I'm free and my spirit will soar to its proper place."

Don't laugh, Suzanne told herself. Here is an Opportunity to Be of Service. She said, "Get in my car, young man. I'll take you wherever you need to go, and I'll listen to you the whole way and never kick you out like your father does. Maybe we'll catch up with him and maybe we won't. I was going to press flowers here for a bit, but probably we both ought to be moving on."

She expected an argument, but he didn't quarrel. Instead, he wandered almost jauntily to the passenger side of the front seat, giving a little hop every time he stepped on his left leg, pulling a pen out of the pouch at his belt and showing off by twirling it deftly between his fingers. Once they were in the car, he clicked it between twirls. Really, it was quite a distraction.

"Tell me a poem, if you're such a poet," she said, to get him to stop. There was some surprising feeling in her stomach, something energizing in an odd way. Here she was driving across a gorge on a two-lane bridge, air on either side and white water below, with a crazed and fragrant poet tapping a pen on the armrest between them. This was quite unusual for her and Phil's kind of life.

"You don't want to hear," Sean Finn said.

"Oh, I do. My husband wrote poems too. I'm a great appreciator."

He snorted. "You're really twisting my arm," he said. "All right then. Ready? This one I call 'Fish':

Fish float belly up
In a roaring river hearse
But never will I drown, o Dad,

In the whirlpool of your curse.
O putrid man, you hook me
With your blasted barb-ed reel—that's with a *e*,
But the real—that's with a *a*—But the real in truth eludes you
And you don't know how I feel."

Well, speak of the devil, if it isn't Phil in a whole nother incarnation, Suzanne said to herself.

"That's my shortest poem," he said. "Here's another one. You have to listen up close, now. You listening?"

They'd left the bridge behind. It was starting to warm up. She might have to roll down the window in a bit. Then there'd be that long drive across the desert. Enjoy the cool while you can. "I'm listening," she said.

"It's titled 'Gadarene.' You know the Gadarenes?"

"I'm not exactly illiterate," she said, and would have said "unlike you" except obviously he did know how to put a few words together one after the other. "Refresh my memory," she said.

"You know Jesus?"

"I thought we went through that back at the lodge," she said, mentally bracing herself to share the first principles of the Only True Gospel then and there.

"In the country of the Gadarenes was where the man lived who had evil spirits. Jesus stuck them evil spirits in the swine, remember?"

"Those," she said. She couldn't help it.

"Them," he said in a tone she didn't regard very highly. Really, if her children had ever talked back like that, she'd have smacked them, and Phil would have backed her up. "Remember them Gadarene swine?"

"Okay, okay," she said. "I do now. You're reminding me of a lot of things." Like, don't ever pick up hitchhikers, even if they're the neglected children of drunk barbarians. Where's a place to stop and let this smart-aleck out? She started to notice there wasn't room for much of a shoulder on the road, let alone a turnaround or a spot for a scenic photo. Well, everything was all right for the moment. Although she did slow down to 35 in case an opportunity presented itself.

"So listen up," he said. Now he was tapping the dash with that pen, hitting it on the accented words.

"Gadarenes

> I can't see how you bear to be
> Bunched up in limbs so hard for me.
> The neck and crotch are wrong, I swear—
> A pig's skin is more mine to wear.
> That wretched peaceful face—I mean Jesus—you know,
>   sometimes those pictures of Jesus lookin' all sympa-
>   thetic just about make me puke—
> That wretched peaceful face—what sham!—
> Says he knows better what I am.
> We pigs that straddle Gadarene air
> Find human bodilessness fair!"

He began to cough. Suzanne took a hand off the wheel to pound his back and offer him a drink from the Dasani bottle she kept stowed under her seat. At last he exhaled.

"That's it," he said.

"That's the end?"

"Couldn't you tell?"

"I got confused, is all," Suzanne tried to mollify him. "When you coughed I didn't think you were done. You really should stop smoking, you know." It was a gamble, but she felt like she had to say it.

The boy heaved back against the headrest. "Oh, Lordy, that does it."

"Does what?" She thought she could see a turnaround up ahead, on one of the switchbacks. She got ready to take advantage and nearly jumped when he groaned.

"What's the matter?"

"I cannot figure out how everyone has such a hard time comprehending my good intentions," he said on a note of high grievance. "Being human is such a burden!—that's what the poem says. Can't you tell? Even being a pig is better. At least if you were one of those pigs, you could sort of fly. Can't anybody tell?" He jabbed the padded dash with the point of his pen: can't anybody *thud*, can't anybody *thud*?

"Young man, you stop that this instant," Suzanne said. "My husband wrote poems, too, and I'm not stupid, but really you are going to put holes in my car, and I will not have that kind of behavior, now or ever."

"Well, I *am* sorry." He flipped the pen around and tapped the clicker end against the dash. "But you know, ma'am, you put a hole in ours."

For two seconds, Suzanne was speechless. Then she saw the sign for the lookout, said, "I didn't mean to," and felt the pen poke her in the rib.

"Stop that!" she cried.

He shrugged and clicked the pen so the point retracted. "Did you say your husband wrote poems?" He acted like he hadn't just done something downright disrespectful. Like he didn't even know it. Probably he didn't. If Phil were alive, they would both teach this boy a thing or two.

"My husband just died," she said, slowing down and signaling. "Put that pen away this minute. We're stopping here to see the view."

"Is all you have left is this Chevy full of presses?" He jerked the pen over his shoulder. She gnashed her teeth at the double "is." "His poems back there? Yeah. Stop."

She already had.

"A perfect spot," he said.

"Yes, it is," she said firmly. You had to take the upper hand. "We can see three states from here. Seven thousand feet up." She turned off the ignition and took the keys out, anchoring them inside her fist. "We haven't found your dad yet," she said. "But you're going to wait right here for him. I need to be on my way, and I will not have you jabbing me or my car for one more second."

"Well, we're all on our way to the Promised Land," he said. He pushed open the door and put one foot on the ground out-side. "No matter," he said. "They all let me out somewhere right around here anyway."

They all?

"That's fine," he said. "Savin' Sam always finds me sometime. It's always the same." He sighed heavily. She really wished he hadn't sighed like that.

"I'll wait with you here for a few minutes," she said sternly. "But that's all. Now go on, get out."

He did. He turned around, though, and put one stained hand on the top of the car and one fray-sandaled foot on the running board, and he thrust his head back toward her through the open door. "Say," he said. "How about I read a few of your husband's poems? While we wait?"

"No," she said. "They're not really any good." In a fit of honesty and kindness she heard herself say, "Yours are better. You use words better."

"Really?" He let out a tiny half-grin of what she thought was flabbergasted pleasure. Maybe. His teeth were brown from the nicotine, or from whatever else she didn't even want to think about, but she thought if he would take care of himself, he might possibly be appealing.

"Can I see?" He reached over the seat and dragged forward by one flap the nearest cardboard box. He fished clumsily inside and pulled out one of the albums. She heard it rip.

"Careful," she said. But she wasn't exactly mad.

"*'Tis the light in your eyes takes me back to my youth,*" he read, one knee on the passenger seat, the other leg still outside the car, holding the album in the space between the headrests. He squinted over at Suzanne, whose face was inches from his. "Hmm," he said. "I think this guy's verse is a little—uncouth."

"Oh, you should be nice," she said, batting at his arm without even thinking about it. A little teasing never hurt anybody. "It's only fair."

"Yeah," he said, and turned the page. "*If marigolds were money and the moon were made of cheese …*" These lines were, she knew by heart, in orange calligraphy on a page of pressed yellow annuals. They'd planted them year after year to keep the bugs away from the roses, but the truth was the Miss Flippins didn't press as nicely as the marigolds. Too many petals.

"'*If the moon were made of cheese*'?" Sean Finn laughed, an amused laugh, not a mean one. "And he rhymes it with 'bees.' Geez."

"Don't swear," she said automatically. Just when she was finding a reason to like him.

"I'll tell you what, old lady, I can do just what I *please*," he said.

"I heard that rhyme." She chose to ignore the tone. Phil always said playful had a better effect than snappish.

The boy pulled the box up over the seat, where it fell clumsily so that two or three of the albums fell out of the box and onto the asphalt, and she must have parked a little closer to the cliff than she'd thought because—did Sean Finn kick them, or was that her imagination?—these albums took a couple of tumbles toward and then over the edge, under the guard rail, pages fluttering, petals like snowflakes, drifting toward Nevada and Idaho and Salt Lake City.

"Whoops," the boy said.

Good-bye, Phil. Good-bye.

Did Sean Finn say these words? How could he? How did he know Phil's name? She couldn't believe he said that. Nor could she quite believe it when he slammed the door, brushed his hands off, said "Thanks, old lady, that was fun," and sauntered off toward the Winnebago, just then pulling up behind them in a one-eyed wobble of dust.

Maybe the most unbelievable thing was what she cried out just then—was it "Wait!" or "Don't leave yet!" or something else? Because then the 'bago stopped, and suddenly they were all heaving boxes, presses, flowers, notebooks into some breach she hadn't realized could open up so deep or so wide, and then she followed that RV all the way to Salt Lake City, those two crazy people gesturing at each other and at her in her rearview mirror, stopping for gas at the same podunk stations, eating lunch and dinner at the same roadside diners, Winnemucca, Elko, Wendover—that whole boring desert they stayed together. Most of the day, the comfort of it just plain shocked her.

Still and all, when she pulled away to take the turnoff from I-15 and they followed her, she had a moment of terror which didn't let up until they roared past, waving, as she drove into Paul's wide driveway up there in ritzy Federal Heights while the sun set in an orange glory over the Great Salt Lake to the west.

Paul, waiting for her on the porch with Katie (Suzanne had called from Tooele to say how close she was), said, "Guardian angels?"

"Gadarene angels. Exactly."

"Cute boy," said Katie. She was seventeen too.

"You couldn't really see him, honey," Suzanne said. "You might not like him closer up." Then she let her mind go back to the turnout at the summit, the impulse that had seemed so right at the time. "But I guess he can work hard when he's a mind to." Katie raised her eyebrows. She'd gotten so pretty since last time. Too bad about her mother, that's what Suzanne always said.

"Let me get your luggage," Paul said. He opened the back gate and stepped back, puzzled. "Where's your stuff, Zan? Weren't you coming back to—I don't know, what did you say, get organized and stay awhile? Wasn't that what you said?"

"I thought the car'd be lighter without it," she said. "My over-night bag's behind the front seat. All I've got." Did Katie look relieved? Suzanne glanced casually up and down the street. Though there was no physical sign of the RV, she had a funny feeling in her stomach, half fear, half promise. She thought she caught a whiff of smoke, a glimpse of yellowed fingertips, a vehicle one-eyed and wobbly just ahead of her, steering straight for the edge of the future, cliffs of a right unpredictable fate.

Incident in a Schoolyard

1996

KATIE MAYNARD ERASES THE BLACKBOARD. EQUATIONS from Adela's lessons dissolve to dust under her cloth, circular and slow deletions she wishes she could apply to Leeny, the problem child in the corner whose mother has come bursting into the classroom after school to plead with the math teacher. But not, Katie knows, because of math. Adela Suaros—Assistant Director of Energy Education Experimental School for Children ("Using the human energy field to enrich learning," says the plaque on the wall in every room), second in command only to Katie's mother, Riva—solves problems not only of addition and subtraction but also of souls divided, in need of repair. She is a master soother. Riva always leaves the hard stuff to Adela. When Riva can't contain a student's energy—when she can't endure even her own daughter's demands, which is practically always, if you ask Katie—she hands the matter over to Adela. "Take care of this, won't you?" Thus Katie erases Adela's blackboards nearly every day.

Now Leeny hunches over her back-corner table, mute in her puckered muslin pinafore, chin tucked down on her chest, stubby forefinger sliding on the workspace's shiny surface, tracing an invisible map of her mother's ramrod-straight path from the door to Adela's desk. Ramrod, that is, in the physical dimension. On the energetic level, Mrs. Lubbock jackknifes all over the room, a flibbertigibbet of upset as chaotic as the colorless hair springing from the loose bun on the back of her head. Even with her back to the scene, Katie can see that, or rather feel it. She's

Riva's daughter. She hardly needs hours of practicum or theory to read what's obvious. Leeny's mother is about to explode in hysteria, and helpless Leeny, in the corner, knows she's somehow the cause.

For the second time, Adela assures Mrs. Lubbock that everyone at Energy Education—teachers, aides, other students, especially Riva, the director—*everyone* is more than competent to support Sarah Eileen through her difficulties. "With poise, Mrs. Lubbock, and heart," she says. "Leeny's limitations are not a problem. Believe me, she's in the right place."

"Can I leave her here, then?" Katie sneaks a look over her shoulder, still swiping the blackboard with the dusty rag. Leeny's mother rocks on her feet between Adela's tidy desk and the classroom's low tables, her trajectory curtailed by her skirt's restricting hem. Or maybe simply by exhaustion.

"Of course. No one's asking her to withdraw."

"That's not what I mean. What I really need to know is, can she stay after school?"

"Peggy—Mrs. Lubbock—of course she can," Adela says. (Katie doesn't stare, but she can feel Adela diffusing the peaks and valleys of panic, spreading out her own calm consciousness to override the mother's agitation.) "We offer after-school classes every second Tuesday."

"Every day," the woman says, hugging herself, breathing hard as she shifts from foot to foot.

The blackboard is clean. Katie turns and leans against it, watching quietly. She knows not to disturb the work. Mrs. Lubbock—Peggy—comes in frequently, sometimes to ask for an exception to some test or other (Leeny is eleven, but only in fourth grade); sometimes to clarify an assignment (math and language arts are especially hard); sometimes, it seems to Katie, simply to use up time. This "every day" is a new demand. Adela repeats back what she understands: "You're asking for a safe place for Leeny to stay."

"Yes, that's it! Thank you so much!"

But the woman's relief is premature. The school is not a day-care. Katie can almost hear Adela (or Riva) say it. "We can't—we don't—"

Before Adela can complete her sentence, Mrs. Lubbock clutches melodramatically at her own chest, bunching up the gray cotton sweater and screwing her mouth into an inconsolable *o*.

Katie has her own ideas about why the woman's so worked up. She's seen Mrs. Lubbock around town—on Temple Square walking among the flower gardens, or at Sam Weller's buying outdated editions of early Joseph Smith books—always with that heavy-handed husband of hers and that other long-skirted woman, with or without children in tow, rarely looking happy. They don't look—anything.

They don't have to. Everyone knows who they are. They and their ilk are in the news from time to time for one or another oddity of behavior, and besides, they dress to call attention to themselves. They're a phenomenon only a little more peculiar (because they didn't kowtow to national demands about monogamy) than the dominant religion their forebears defected from a hundred years ago. That history's part of the ambience, the local color Katie's been trying to explain to Sean.

Sean!

Now, *he's* an enigma. Katie's thoughts careen from the schoolroom to Sean, the new person in her life, the evangelist's kid her aunt found—hitchhiking, was it?—from California. He's taken up most of the space in her consciousness since he arrived. He seems as much of a misfit as Leeny, refusing to go to school, muttering around her father's house, taking long walks with her in the late spring evenings, and hyperbolizing so she can't tell whether to laugh or run away in terror. He says Salt Lake City is a utopian dream gone wrong. He says her parents' marriage is a victim of the city's mystical origins, her father's orthodoxy so at odds with her mother's magical thinking they were bound from the beginning to implode. This frightens Katie a little, since she's often thought much the same thing. But she's kept it to herself until now. Until now, nobody's asked.

And if anyone asked her right now, she'd say in a heartbeat she thinks Leeny is another blowup waiting to happen. She can't be helped, not even if she stays after school once a week or every day. Her tyrant of a father (he's probably her uncle, too) browbeats all the women in his little compound. The whole valley talks about it. And poor trembling Mrs. Lubbock thinks Adela can save her and Leeny from their fate.

The baffling thing is, Riva thinks so too.

And here she is, Riva, Katie's mother, materializing in the doorway like a divine messenger bringing the Word to the troubled earth. Katie sidles from the whiteboard to the math cabinet to sort out the red and blue Montessori rods and gold bead frames Adela uses alternately with computers. Gold beads! Energy! The oddities they employ here! Katie turns her back to the room once more, stilling herself to make her body language neutral.

"How are you, Peggy?" Though she's focused on the math drawers, Katie knows that Riva goes swiftly to Mrs. Lubbock, embracing her, asking after her as if no one is more important, nothing more pressing than the matter at hand. Mrs. Lubbock steps in close. Riva's arm, lean and strong in her navy silk suit, encircles the shoulders of the polygamist's wife. "Is your new job working for you, Peggy? How are the other children?"

"They're making out," Leeny's mother says tiredly.

"Excellent," Riva says, encouraging her to go on. "And—?"

"We'll be okay if I can stay at the Z.C.—at least we have food. And the electricity's back on."

"If you can stay?" Riva is puzzled. "Is the store firing you?"

"No. No. Not them. Keifer." Mrs. Lubbock's voice is shrill. "If he gets money from the city, he says I have to quit."

After a pause, Riva says, "Dela? Would you come here, please?"

Katie hears Adela stepping in close to join the conversation, which continues in a murmur, all of them tuned to a secret, private vibe.

As usual.

"You hate her," Sean said just this morning as he dropped in beside her as if by coincidence, matching his steps to hers casually on the way down the hill to East High. "Your mom. She doesn't get you. She barely even knows you're there. You feel a screamatory urge to smash the ties. Right? Am I right?"

Oh, is he right. *He* knows she's there. To walk the blocks with him is to play notes in the same chord, hum on the same instrument. She wants to drown in his melody, resonate with him up and down the scale.

"And it's not just your mom, it's your dad, too. I can tell." He's a year older than she is. He does know. She's sure of it.

"So," he says, out of the blue like that, "tell me about polygamy." Everybody's fascinated by polygamy when they come to Salt Lake City. It's the one thing everybody seems to know about the Mormons. If they only knew the Lubbocks!

"It's complicated," she said.

"Everything's complicated, sweetie," he said, running a finger down her arm.

Doesn't she know it. But back to the polygamists.

Katie would never say, as her mother just has, that any slice of Peggy Lubbock's shabby life is excellent. She'd say, "What did you marry that creep for in the first place, if he already had a wife?" She'd say, "Why do you stick around when he hits you if you do anything he doesn't like?" She'd say, "How can you stand to live off crunchy brown bread made from storage wheat? Or wear long skirts from thrift shops all year long?" But she knows—Paul, her dad, from whom Riva is long estranged, and Adela, who tells Katie things Riva ought to tell her but never does, have both said that according to the Lubbocks' belief system, plural marriage is a divine practice with serious spiritual brownie points. Another thing Katie knows is that her own great-grandparents were polygamists, faithful and true clear up until the Manifesto forbade the practice in 1890 so Utah could join the Union.

The last interesting, complicated thing she knows is that Mr. Lubbock himself would condemn Riva to eternal hell if he knew *her* private life. Plural marriage may be the road to life everlasting, but leaving your husband for a woman? Not okay. Not by Katie, not by Paul, and not by Lubbock. So there's something they have in common, she and Lubbock. Yet there's Riva, conspiring with Adela right now to save Mrs. Lubbock and Leeny. Boy, are things complicated.

Now in the schoolroom, Katie keeps her energy quiet and invisible, sealed and smooth, arranging the colored beads and tubes carefully so that none of these thoughts are revealed while her mother and Adela commiserate with Mrs. Lubbock, the gist of every utterance falling beyond Katie's hearing.

"Can't you—?"

"If she—"

"We would—"

"It's only—"

"She won't—"

"I'll try—"

"Thank you …"

When it stops, Katie quietly turns partway to watch them hug. Riva squeezes Mrs. Lubbock's bony hand. Adela helps Leeny into the shabby corduroy shirt that passes for a jacket. Together they zip books, pencils, papers into the child's backpack. "See you tomorrow," Mrs. Lubbock says, sounding less like she might give up the ghost any minute. "'See you tomorrow, teacher,' say that, Leeny, 'I'll be here tomorrow while Mama finishes work up at the big store downtown …'"

Riva goes with them into the hall, holding Leeny's hand, her arm again around Mrs. Lubbock's shoulders. In the classroom, Adela putters. She adjusts the blinds at the windows, transfers chalk from the blackboard tray to her desk drawer, moves Leeny's chair so it sits straight against the table. Finally, she meets Katie at the math cupboard.

"You know 'the poor and the needy'?" She always knows what Katie's thinking. When Sean knows what she's thinking, it's scary. He's new, and he's young, and he's a boy. But with Adela, it's usually a relief. "The Lubbocks are them."

"The poor and the needy? You think?"

"Yes," says Adela. "Riva cares about their welfare."

"Somebody should call the police on Mr. Lubbock."

Adela shrugs, barely. "Somebody might have to, eventually. I'm not so sure we're the ones to do it."

"Oh, they'd both love you if you did it," Katie says. "Riva—okay, Mom—and Mrs. Lubbock. They both think everything you do is perfect. Besides what's-her-name, you're the only person Riva pays any attention to."

Adela laughs a little sadly. "I don't know," she says. "I know she ought to pay more attention to you, Katie-girl." She fingers the tendril coiling at Katie's ear. "Well, I don't have any answers, in the case of the Lubbocks. Come on, I'll drive you to your house, drop in and see how your dad's doing. That boy Sean still hanging around?" She leaves the classroom door open—she always does, for air, she says—and they move toward the parking lot, ready to go home.

IN THE HIGH-END BENCH NEIGHBORHOOD OF FEDERAL Heights, the view west across the valley to the Great Salt Lake is equaled, in its power to take away the breath, only by the view of the granite crags of the Wasatch Mountains to the east and south. Twice now Sean's been admonished not to smoke in the house if he must indulge at all, so he walks with Katie in the evenings, partly so he can drag on a Lucky, but mostly to philosophize. To the west, layers of hot, dry air flow above a city wrested from saline desert and sagebrush. During the winter months, the upthrust igneous barrier of the Wasatch Front catches and holds in its frozen heights whatever moisture streams in from the north and west, transforming it into powdery dry crystals of snow and ice, drifting laminae of the greatest snow on earth. These recede in spring, yielding delicate wildflower fields, whose multifarious blooms cycle quietly according to mysteries of elevation, length of day, time of year—ancient, timeless patterns. Some years ago, a few miles south, the polygamous child bride of a self-proclaimed prophet strode into a naturopathic clinic and shot its director point-blank seven times at her husband's behest. She did this because she was covenanted to obey her man, who perceived that the doctor threatened his omnipotence. Walking and talking here together, Sean and Katie crisscross histories and secret truths, patterns as old as the mountains have been occupied. She tries to explain.

"My dad's an elder. Also a teacher. But he doesn't make his living in the Church." Katie waves at stately brick houses a hundred years old, refurbished for the end of the twentieth century, with their well-established stands of trees, generations of conscientious flower gardens, gazebos in yards behind wrought iron fences. When Riva chose Nina, Paul moved here from the Avenues, not a sacrifice but a movement toward healing. Katie means for Sean to understand the differences between her father and his, why her father is good, why he doesn't complain, why he'll take Sean in till a foster home is found. "He just—serves. It's what you do."

"What good is that, Katie-o?" He taps the ashes against the trunk of the blue spruce on the sidewalk edge of the stake president's yard. "If you're not getting paid, why spend your time doing stuff for fools too stupid to do it for themselves?"

"They're not stupid. You have to have compassion. My father says *you* deserve compassion."

He rolls his eyes, blowing out a stream of smoke. "So much he knows. I thought you said he never pays attention to you. Or your brother."

"Oh, he pays attention to Chris," Katie says. "He wants Chris to go on his mission. He'll do anything to make sure of that."

Sean waves that away, wheezing, a sound she's come to recognize as a prelude to soapboxing. "I share your pain, Katie-girl. Our parents did us no favors by bearing us. Deserting mothers! Neglectful fathers! They put us in the 'naught' column. We were born only to drag in the dust behind their choices of conflict and rue." He sweeps off his Oakland A's baseball cap for effect, replaces it backward on his sandy shag of hair.

She laughs, partly at his overwrought diction, partly to suppress a certain discomfort.

"Your dad tries to hide in his 'service,' but your mom—she just pushes you aside. No wonder you hate her."

"Not supposed to hate," she says automatically. This is familiar territory. She knows the correct things to say. "Didn't your preacher dad ever tell you that? It's in the Bible. He should know."

"Sorry, Katie-o, but my dad's a whited sepulchre. He may say don't fornicate and lie, but oh, Lordy, my oh my. That's all he does. And I don't even have a mom. 'Don't hate'? That's exactly what my life's been leading to." He leans against the Butterfields' stone fence, gray and reddish river stones so old and smooth they might have been—probably were—brought here by Butterfield ancestors from across the plains in 1847. Sean's cigarette butt leaves smoky smudges on the overlaid surface. Ashes scatter into the lush and shaded lawn below.

"You don't have to like Riva just because she *bore* you. Do I have to remind you? She leaves you when you're a baby, then hires you as a lackey in her *energy* school and doesn't even talk to you. Pays more attention to them—what are they? Pluralist p'lygs? We've got a lot in common, Katie-o. We've been dumped on. And we must dump them back. An eye for an eye."

Tossing the last cinders over the fence, he pats his pockets for pack and lighter. "They have no idea what it means to be family. To be *our* family. They deserve what they get—and what they get is *blastisssimo!*" He flicks his cigarette lighter in that way he has, so that a hissing flame shoots into the air. She jumps, but she also stares, fascinated by his blatant disregard for principle. Sean runs his forefinger through the flame, then touches the corner of her eye with a proprietary lingering. "Sss," he says. "You and I—we deserve—sssatisfaction. Fantastisssimo."

She sinks into him, her brain roaring because she is barely seventeen and he is fascinating. "You can't even imagine how I feel sometimes."

"Yes, I can," he says, leaning into her face, covering her mouth with burning lips. When he pulls away, her face is on fire. "Oh, yesss I can."

AT HOME IN HOLLADAY, RETIRED AT THE END OF THE DAY with Riva to the studio behind the house they share, Nina drops a lump of ochre clay onto the slurry table. New mud dapples the concentric rings of old stains on the maple slab and spatters her apron, pale brown from years of handbuilding close to the body. "Adela agreed?" she says, settling herself in the old director's chair and turning the lump clockwise between strong palms.

"Of course," Riva says. "She sees what's going on with the Lubbocks as plainly as I do."

"You ask a lot, love." Nina screws clay-thickened thumbs into ridges that will become shoulder and lip, if all goes well.

"And why shouldn't I? Who will help Peggy if we don't?" Riva's fingers slide over the series of unfired urns on the shelf beside the door. "You haven't seen her lately. Another huge bruise on her arm." She describes it with her thumb and middle finger. "That man's a monster. And the child has to have somewhere to go."

"So you'll protect her and her daughter indefinitely." Nina dips her hand in the tray of water nailed to the side of the table, shakes her fingers, and starts again on the lopsided form, teasing out the grace hiding in the rough material. They've been together the richest years of their mutual forty-two, sharing bed and home fire and practically every thought. They wear each other's rings, rose and white and yellow gold braided together in Celtic knots like their interlaced hearts, never removing them even to make pots or garden in the deep black soil behind the studio. So Nina does not blurt, *You overcompensate for ills you blame the Church for, crimes against you and other women. You think you can judge, punish, and modify the Church, and save those who've been wronged. You're wasting your precious energy, Riva, your precious Energy Ed.* Instead, her fingers keep on kneading, thrust so deep in the clayey heart her knuckles cannot be seen.

"I won't abandon her." Riva strokes a lopsided piece of greenware. "Any more than you'd abandon this."

"I'd abandon it the second I put myself or you in danger by keeping on," Nina says, not looking up, pressing and turning with curved palm and fingers. "Let Social Services help. You can't atone for a whole society's sins."

Riva nudges the one-sided piece, letting it wobble in a semicircle before she taps it off the shelf, catching it just before it crashes. "I have to try. That's who I am, remember?"

After a minute, Nina says, "In two weeks, school's out. Plan some end-of-the-year after-school thing for children and parents so it's not just you or Adela waste—working with Leeny alone every afternoon. Involve everyone. Don't make her a special case."

Riva palms smooth the thick dark tendrils around Nina's ears. "A carnival," she says. "Recruit parents to volunteer and plan."

"Celebrate three years of Energy Ed."

"Good. You can do it. It's only two more weeks."

The thing they both know for sure is, Riva will not forsake the polygamist's wife. Will pour energy into the project till something tells her to stop. Not before. Not one moment before.

"TWO LETTERS HAVE BEEN SENT ALREADY."

Paul Maynard, president and CEO of M & L Construction, oldest and most venerable developer in the Salt Lake Valley, maintains a certain good-humored dignity. Bent a bit at the waist so that his stomach will stay calm and his voice will project, he stands at the edge of a sea of plastic trikes, dog feces, and clothes poles like mainmasts hung with underwear and baby blankets. The long-skirted woman on the other side of this vast expanse makes no response, except to reach with her free arm toward the two mid-sized children kicking a green ball to each other with more force than the space allows, so that one of them has to run after the ball when their mother, or whoever she is, gestures for them to stop. Paul watches as she pats their overall-clad bottoms, murmuring to them, he presumes, to go inside. She adjusts the toddler on her hip, hitches her skirt, and floats toward him with a grace it's easy to smile at despite his errand. Modern young mothers in their flip-flops and jeans don't sashay like this any more. They more generally bluster, or else they ignore him, as Katie has begun to do, to the detriment of his gastritis. He could hardly say whether his teenaged daughter glides or swaggers any more. She's less and less in his line of sight.

But this woman—self-possessed, with her tidy brown braid and straightforward blue eyes, apparently willing to deal with him head on—skims the chaos in the yard with barely a glance. "I'm sorry," she says when they're face to face. She wipes a hand on her clean, ironed apron to hold out to him deferentially. "What were the letters about?"

He shakes her hand—rough skin, with a firmness he appreciates—and transfers his card to her care. "Mrs. Lubbock?" he asks.

Her smile warms his gut. "The first," she says, glancing down and back up at him. She doesn't know what he's here for, he realizes. "I'm Jean. Which of us would you like?"

"Ah." He remembers another Jean, also tied to polygamists—his own grandma, child of polygamists, just like so many early Salt Lake natives. Riva always liked her, the only thing about him she seems to have enjoyed. She died weeks before Katie was born. He has wondered—he stops himself. "Actually, I need to talk to Mr. Lubbock, if he's home," Paul says.

Jean Lubbock cocks her head at him, settling the baby, who's beginning to fuss.

"We've sent a couple of letters already about the condominium project going up in this block. An access road will pass through the southeast corner here, cutting your plot by less than a quarter of an acre. You'll be paid well for the easement."

Now she shakes her head. "I don't think so," she says.

He coughs politely, swallowing against the taste of bile, and starts again. "We'll start excavating early in July. The letters outline the county's strategy to reimburse you for the easement. It's a fair settlement. I'm here to make sure the letters have been received and the information is clear. Has your husband said anything to you about this?"

She looks back at the house. Tucking the card in her mouth, she shifts the child to her other hip, grimacing as if the weight— of the child or of the problem—bothers her.

"Mr.—" she checks the card—"Maynard," she says, "I don't think you understand the situation here."

He's heard this gambit before. It never bodes a happy conclusion. The acid smell of wet diaper begins to intrude on his courtesy.

"Mrs. Lubbock," he says, "I'm not sure who doesn't understand whom. Let me ask again: is your husband at home?"

The woman's looks do not belie her age, he realizes as her hesitation mounts. She is genuinely young, though the fullness of her breasts and hips suggests she's endured several pregnancies already, perhaps with little time between. And the flash of defiance on her face is adolescent.

"He's not—he doesn't—I'd advise you not to bother him," she says. "I told you, you don't understand. We're two whole families. We live peacefully together, on this land."

"I understand," he says. He does, too. In the beginning, polygamy was the basis of a Zion society, family, covenants, eternal ties. Security forever. Paul has often thought his family's ulcers, or whatever the stomach trouble is, began when Zion never came to pass. The Lubbocks still believe it will.

"We take care of ourselves," the woman says, smoothing the wavy blond hair on her boy's forehead, on his neck, on his forehead again. "We don't need an easement. It's dangerous. We have eleven children here. They don't need a road through their yard."

"I'm sorry," he says, trying to appear as well-meaning as possible, standing not too stiffly in his navy suit and tie despite his discomfort, making sure his voice is not too loud. "However, this isn't an option we're offering you. It's a notification. Can you see that?" He even reaches out for the child's hand, but the boy whimpers into his mother's neck and pulls his fist toward his mouth, where his thumb goes straightaway. The second Mrs. Lubbock fixes her jaw.

"All right," she says. "I'll get Keifer. But I wish you'd leave us alone. We have enough problems without your interference." She turns away. Even moving fast, she's still graceful. Paul has time to recognize within himself a certain admiration for the upbringing that teaches that willingness to move beautifully even under these conditions.

Then Keifer Lubbock slams the door open through which his first wife disappeared a moment ago. He must have been waiting on the other side of it. A big man, not tall but well-fed and conspicuously muscular. He ambles across the yard, kicking aside a trike as if it were a pebble. The sleeves of his gray cotton shirt are rolled to his thick biceps, his heavy arms and wrists covered with coarse hair, his jeans held tight around his bulky waist by a woven rope with a carabiner buckle. His beard, Paul notes, needs trimming. His rheumy eyes bear down on Paul with animosity.

"Keifer Lubbock," he says. "You Maynard?"

Paul offers his hand. Lubbock glances at it, his lip drawn back.

"You aware this is private property? Wholly owned? For a hundred and thirteen years?"

"You've received the letters, signed by the county attorney and the developers of the land on the five acres up the block, toward the canyon?"

"That's what I'm saying," Lubbock says. "You're not offerin' near enough. We need the land. You got to pay us more than you're saying. Understand?"

Paul wishes there weren't stubble on his chin, a rope belt around his waist. He wishes Lubbock weren't so stereotypically anachronistic, so belligerent, so blustery. But at least he's not one of those skinny twenty-two-year-old boys coming out of such houses as this with little besides a tufty beard and high-pitched, hesitant, ungrammatical speech. Paul doesn't know where all the children end up. He knows of a few who've gone mainstream, but most of them, home-schooled in reactionary subjects like the sacred holiness of the Constitution and their own brand of nineteenth-century religion, blend into the underground culture and show up with their own trains of wives and children in Hilldale or Colorado City or one of their other cities in the Rocky Mountain West, outlandish and isolated. What appeal could their archaic philosophy possibly have beyond an obsolete loyalty to long-dead experimenters? Paul catches himself. At least Lubbock is an adult. And presumably literate.

Paul pulls another copy of the letter from his inside breast pocket and removes it from its officially-addressed envelope.

"The terms are set out clearly here," he says, pointing. "Second paragraph. We'll need your assent by July first. A check will be prepared the day we receive your signature for more than enough to improve what's left of your holdings. We'd appreciate your cooperation." He offers his hand again.

"You got any idea who you're talking to?" Lubbock steps forward, his nose inches from Paul's.

Paul moves back, willing the bile to stay down. "Mr. Lubbock. The next individual who visits here in regard to this matter will be an attorney. After that may come officers of the law.

I'm merely here to be sure you're aware of terms and conditions. May I assume so?"

Lubbock balls his fist and swings. Paul moves quickly, right and back, an effective dodge followed by a quick drop of the letter onto the dusty ground when Lubbock swings again. Paul turns on his heel and makes his way—moderate pace, he mutters to himself, keep your eyes down, don't rush—back to the company Lexus outside the barbed wire fence.

Before he can open the door, though, Lubbock gives chase. Acid swirls into Paul's throat before he realizes that Lubbock isn't running after him but past, to the rust-patched minivan parked four or five strides behind the LS 400. The driver must have stopped there when she saw them talking, wanting to stay out of sight, or out of reach. The family's patriarch wrenches open her door, bellowing. She shouts something—she ducks—he pounds the front of the Caravan as he bolts across its path and slides back the side panel with a bang. He reaches in, grabs a child and pulls her from her rear seat.

"Where you been?" he roars. "Maybe you'll tell me if your mother won't—we been looking everywhere for you—girl—you belong at home helping your family—don't think you can get away—" The child cowers, one arm flung up to defend her head. Her mother leaps from her perch behind the wheel, running clumsily around the back of the minivan to protect her daughter from her husband's blows.

Paul puts one foot on the dusty earth beneath the door of his Lexus. "Mr. Lubbock," he protests, beginning to stand, but the minivan inches forward, driverless, quickly gaining speed, and Paul sees that he must move his car *now* if it is not to be rear-ended, so he slides adroitly back onto the leather seat, snapping the key in the ignition as he yanks the door closed and pulls smoothly into the gravel road, a plume of dust feathers in his wake. The minivan meanders in the haze, as if perplexed, and swerves hard left into the yard, crushing the fallen envelope.

In Paul's rear-view mirror, the woman drags at a gray shirt cuff while the father pummels the truant daughter, harder and smaller until Paul is forced to look forward, not back, pointing his vehicle down the canyon, scrabbling in the glove box for antacids, his stomach a ruin of rage and dismay.

AFTER SCHOOL, THE HALLS OF ENERGY EDUCATION ARE quiet and warm. Katie likes the hour or so she spends there alone with Adela while they put to rights the empty math space and the silently breathing library. The absence of children echoes in the halls like a waterfall at the end of summer, Stewart Falls up Provo Canyon or Doughnut Falls in Big Cottonwood (perhaps she will take Sean to one or the other of these, if she can get Suzanne to drive them), a soothing trickle instead of a torrent. She worried after yesterday that, with Adela babysitting Leeny, she'd be sent home, but apparently not. Instead, the three of them, Leeny and Adela and Katie, are in the main office printing off posters to tape up on the bulletin boards and message stations around the corridors and classrooms. The blues and greens of the posters are muted because Riva prefers colors that relax over ones that excite. Vibratory resonance and all that. But in bold block letters, the posters advertise a carnival—in less than two weeks!— which, in Katie's experience, is a fairly high-energy event. She asks Adela under the beat and hum of the color printer what she thinks.

"About the party, or about the posters?" Adela supervises while Leeny, head down and shoulders hunched, draws the oversized sheets from the printer and straightens them, side by parallel side, on the long table under the window.

Katie shrugs. Either one. Both. For years Katie has turned to Adela or Paul to explain things Riva will not, such as the reason for this carnival. And who designed the posters overnight. And why Leeny's face and arm are splotched dark blue and black— although Katie can guess that one. She fervently hopes Mr. Lubbock never shows up at Energy Ed.

Adela rubs Leeny's back gently with one hand. "Good job," she says. "Let's grab the stickum and go hang these, shall we?" Her voice is extra bright. Katie first heard that voice back in the days when she and Carlos and their boy Logan used to show up at the Maynards' every Sunday with a dish of spinach lasagna, regular as church. This was after Riva left, blasting a giant black hole in their never-exactly-sweet-and-light home. That was long before Energy Ed, back when Katie and her brother were small and the grownups heaved all their efforts into pretending everything was normal. Maybe Leeny hasn't figured it out, but to Katie, it's obvious: things are not normal now either.

But now, as then, Adela is good at smoothing over trouble for the afflicted. She takes Leeny's hand, stashes the little pile of posters in her other armpit, and conducts the fourth-grader into the hallway, talking a mile a minute about this and that to keep Leeny distracted, just as she used to do for Katie when she was that age. Katie might tag along, except that at the precise moment those two head down the perpendicular hallway to the lower school classrooms, who should come around the corner from the opposite direction but Riva, the Director herself, propelling the second Mrs. Lubbock by her limp and pallid arm.

Katie grabs a *Utah Education* magazine from the rack by the door, sits far back in the microfiber easy chair, and flips through the pictures of private schools in the story about school choice featured on the cover, as if this were the most urgent issue Katie has to think about today. Riva ushers Peggy Lubbock past her into the back office with only a tiny nod toward Katie. As soon as the two women pass through the half-door to the back office, Katie slides from the comfortable chair by the table to the wooden stool stationed just outside the door. They can't see her, but she can hear them. She listens shamelessly. She knows what she would see, by listening.

"Bring your awareness to the places under my hands," Riva says. "That's right, just close your eyes and breathe there. You're in a crisis—like a baby bird falling from its nest—but you haven't hit the ground yet, there's support, wind beneath your wings. Breathe that air … there you go …"

Katie leans over to risk a glance through the tinted glass in the door. It's just as she figures: the two women sit facing each other on the two rolling stools Riva keeps in her office across from her desk. Katie's mother has placed one of her palms on Mrs. Lubbock's heart, the other on her forehead. Both women's eyes are closed.

"Relax your forehead, your eyebrows, your eyelids … that's it … see yourself helping customers at the Z.C., that's right, see that paycheck taking care of the bills, see yourself independent and whole, your sister-wives thanking you gladly …"

When they're finished, Peggy clings to Riva like a drowning woman. "I could never do it without you," she sobs.

"Of course you could," Riva reassures her, rubbing her back, her neck, her head. Katie pulls back before they open the door. They sweep through without noticing her there, leaning her head against the wall, practicing silence.

DAYS LATER, SEAN AND KATIE STROLL THROUGH THE chain warehouse down in the valley with its layers of tools and home improvement aids rising in a forest of metal racks fifteen feet high on either side. Sean flaps his hands in his army jacket pockets like vulture wings. "Now's our chance. This rope. This gas. These wicky-wicks. It's time to put our money where our mouths are, walk the talk. You can get rid of your mother for good. Show your dad what you think of his rules." He licks his mouth lazily, reaches out to brush her sweater with his knuckle. He is sure of her. "The time is right. Don't weaken. Don't give in to nice-girl now."

"I'm not," she says angrily. "I just don't know." She doesn't want him to suspect she's frightened. They've taken money from her dad's account with his card but without his knowledge, and it has not given her the sense of freedom she expected. "Do we have to have this much gas? Is there another way to do this that doesn't cost so much?"

"Like what?" His voice is mean now, sarcastic and guttural. "You have a better idea? An immediately recent and brilliant new plan that will demonstrate equally graphically our objections to the way we've been brought up?" He squints one eye. "Isn't it a little late?"

She doesn't tell him she has a terrible vision: her father, emerging from a corridor, any corridor, catching them in his sights, knowing their plan precisely without having to ask a word. Nor does she tell him the terror here is not that this might happen, but that she could not choose Sean if it did. She's sure she would crumple beneath her father's steady and principled gaze.

Sean hands her the loop of rope. She gives the cashier a twenty and asks for a bag with the change. On the other side of the cash register, Sean meets her casually; casually, they stroll toward the exit. When they believe no one is watching, he takes the plastic bag with the red logo and saunters in the direction of the restroom. After a bit he returns, ambling listlessly, his baseball cap backward and his pack of cigarettes a square bulge in his jacket pocket, the sack's handles twisted around his wrist, dangling a much heavier load.

"You coming?" he says. She sees how easy it is. She goes.

LEENY CLINGS TO MAMA JEAN, WHO KEEPS ORDER AMONG the littles cooing over balloons and flags, displays and activities, in the playgrounds and halls of Energy Ed. Leeny feels safe, because today, patient Mama Jean, who's nicer than her own mother, is here with the littles. Papa hardly ever slaps her when Mama Jean or the littles are around.

Here, at this school, Energy Education, Adela teaches Leeny every day, repeating over and over the multiplication tables, laying a cool hand against her forehead, making the fours or fives into a song, saying "Good girl" or "Wonderful!" or "That's the way." But lately there has been a ruffle about this, Mama Peggy letting her stay there after all Adela's other students have said goodbye, even Tommy and Bill-boy. Papa slaps her when she comes home, but she couldn't leave any sooner even if she wanted to. Mama Peggy picks her up after work at the Z.C., and they drive to the house singing "Popcorn Popping on the Apricot Tree" and "Jesus Wants Me for a Sunbeam" as happy as ever until they get there and Papa slaps them. Today, Mama Peggy is still at the Z.C., but Mama Jean has come instead, so Leeny feels safe.

Safe enough to peek around her sometimes. School has felt swirly since the first bells rang from the office this morning to signal time to sit in her seat and start learning. Tommy and Bill-boy, who usually perch on either side of her and show her which red or blue rods she should fix on for math, told her instead, this morning, to bring her drawings and glue them, and theirs too, and the other children's, to the windows with stickum. They did that for so long her legs got tired and she had to sit down for a while by the pond. Then when the second bells rang, Adela came to fetch her and navigated her through blue and green and yellow flags twisting in windy spirals from every tree and bush.

Children ran everywhere all day. The air billowed and rushed around and she had to put her head down on her desk so she wouldn't get too confused. Ms. Riva even forgot the third and fourth bells, the ones that signal lunch and end of learning, or else decided not to ring them because mamas and papas began to whirl up the path, fling open the front door for each other to step through, and whisk their children into the yard to play Parachute and Dance Circle and Four-Square. The parents brought dishes of brown cake and round sand cookies and snaky carrot things, and then Mama Jean was there, and so were the littles, bringing cups of minty lemonade that brightened Leeny's mouth.

Now, when she lifts her head up from Mama's skirt, she sees the many children from her school class holding hands with their parents, twirling them in circles from one end of the schoolyard to the other, showing off their drawings and cramming food in their mouths and clapping to the music. There are blue-eyed Petra and black Scotty, running in circles around the trees and down the path to the hedge maze by the water pond. The big girls and boys don't hold their mamas' hands, but their mamas and papas follow them around anyway, more mamas and papas than Leeny has ever seen here before. They talk to each other, laughing among the big trees with the hand-shaped leaves and down to the hedge maze by the blue water and back to the pink and green bushes under the windows.

She tightens her fists in Mama Jean's skirt suddenly, for there comes Papa. He has on his green straw hat, which means going out in public. Mama sees him, too, and pats Leeny's back to hurry her toward him, without making her let go of Mama's skirt. Papa does not usually slap her when Mama Jean is there, she remembers, but it's still hard for her to look up, sunward, into Papa's bearded face. Mama hands him a brown cake and he bites it and picks up one of the littles and keeps walking. Leeny lets go of Mama's skirt and skitters fast to keep up.

There, by the other door, still outside, are some of the bigger students, ones that help in the math classroom sometimes and other ones Leeny doesn't know. They don't speak to her, so she doesn't mind they're there. Adela comes through the door. She speaks to Katie and shakes hands with the tall pointy boy next to Katie that Leeny has never seen before. Then Adela comes all the way over! To Papa!

"Mr. Lubbock?" Adela says in a bright nice voice. "I'm Sarah's teacher. She's doing very well this year—we're so glad to have her."

"Sarah?" Papa sneers. He never calls Leeny Sarah.

"Are you her other mother?" Adela says brightly to Mama Jean, who smiles and nods.

Papa mutters. He touches his fingertip to his hat. He pulls on his beard as he takes his hand down. The boy with Katie stares at Papa, who scowls back. Katie points at Leeny. Adela catches Leeny's hand and tells Papa how Katie helps her teach. Papa nods. "Need all the help you can get with that one, don't you," he says. He grabs Mama Jean by the wrist and keeps walking.

Leeny, glad she's on Mama's other side, takes a little by the hand so he won't get lost, and they clomp down to the hedge maze, which Leeny knows perfectly from going through it a hundred times with Katie and without her. She loosens herself from Mama Jean and shows the littles which turns launch you deeper into the maze and which ones are just more walls of red-leaf hedge that rise up spiky and stop you from going anywhere else. The littles laugh and shout and run in all directions. A long time later, she brings them out the other side. There are Katie and the tall boy, by the water pond, the tips of their noses very close together. Balloons in the trees behind them are red circle portions. Leeny knows this from math.

"Do you see Mama Jean?" Leeny asks Katie. Katie jumps back.

"Whoa, Leeny, you scared me," she says, a little shake in her laugh. "Here, we'll take you."

Leeny and the littles follow Katie and the jagged-edged boy around the outside of the hedge maze till they see Papa and Mama Jean sitting on the wooden bench there. Papa fans himself with his green hat. Mama nurses the baby lying crosswise in her lap with a blue cloth covering his face. Katie and her boy walk the children to the bench. Leeny can't look at Papa, so she sidles around behind the bench to plunge her fingers in Mama Jean's hair, where she'll be safe. The boy, Katie's tall boy, raises his eyebrows. "That's a lot of kidlets, mister," he says to Papa before they drift off back to where they were. "Not easy to take care of 'em all, I bet."

Quick as a snake, Papa stands up and slaps him on the back of the head. The boy flings a fist back smack in the middle of Papa's eyes. Papa's head lurches back and then forward. Leeny pulls her breath in hard and hides her face in Mama's hair. Mama detaches the baby from her breast and rises, not too fast, to pull Papa aside by his sleeve.

"Keifer," she says. "We should go."

Leeny can see the red spot between his eyes, like one of the balloons in the trees. He is so mad he can't talk, like when the car rolled into the yard after Mama Peggy jumped out of it, so mad his face is black even though it's only red. That time, Mama Peggy got slapped. This time, Mama Jean takes Papa by the wrist again, leans down to Leeny to tell her to keep the littles a ways behind, and marches him up the path toward the school building.

Leeny gathers up the littles like one two three four five ducks in a line and follows after. They pass the many children and their mamas and papas laughing in the whirl of red balloons, brown cake and green and blue flags. So that's what a carnival is, Leeny whispers as she helps them climb on the bumper and over the stuck-closed tailgate of Papa's big gray truck, one little after another, heave-ho and over you go. When the truck's engine rumbles, signaling they are going now, she is still helping the last one. With her shoulder, she pushes him, bottom up, into the bed of the truck, and then she jumps herself, but she misses the handle. Oh-oh, she thinks. But she knows she can't catch it. Papa is driving very fast. Her heart beats hard, but she isn't hurt anywhere, just a little burny scrape where she landed on her knee. It's all right, she says to herself. I'll stay in the classroom till Mama comes back for me.

"PUT IT THERE, KATIE-O," SEAN SAYS, POINTING TO THE darkest corner. "Scuttle. Do it."

They have hung around, making themselves invisible, shifting between the maze and the inside classrooms, till the carnival has dissipated, the balloons drooping, one and two families departing at a time, laughing still, congratulating Riva on a great party, three great years, the children waving, the parents happy.

They count on Adela not to see them where they crouch in the maze as she locks the door behind her, the last to go. Her car is out of sight down the block before they scurry to the downstairs custodial closet, as per plan. A phone rings, a machine picks up—"Hello? We're looking for Sarah Eileen"—and then the hall is stone quiet, the percolating babble of the afternoon a mere echo, a whisper, a nothing-at-all in the empty building. Perfect.

Two brooms—one to sweep with, one to push leaves around the yard—hang like dead men from nails in the wall. A yarn mop stands warily dry in its bucket. Goosenecked bottles of naturally derived, biodegradable surfactants line the sterile floor where Katie drops the frayed end of the gas-drenched rope coil. Sean kicks it to the back, feeds out line, threads it under the door as he wedges the half-gate shut. Gripping the back of her arm, his knuckles brush her breast so that she is wet and breathless, not just with their errand but with the promise of more from him later. He propels them both around the corner to the bottom of the stairs and pushes her up before him.

"Wait a second," she says, but his hand on her buttock presses her relentlessly up.

"Go," he says.

The rope unwinds behind them, thirteen bare steps to the main floor, dark windows facing south, away from the street lights, so that the announcement-laden bulletin boards are hard to see. They both know what they say: Anniversary Carnival! Come One, Come All! Displays! Games! Pageantry!

"Your mother so lacks subtlety," Sean says. He's been mean since the polygamist hit him.

"You're not exactly a paragon of subtlety yourself," she reminds him. "It's your own fault."

"That guy is my father all over again," he snarls. "I hate 'im. But I got 'im. We'll get 'em all, Katie-o. We'll get 'em all."

The rope reeks of its regular-gas bath, siphoned from the Sinclair pump down the road while they filled up Paul's Lexus, but no one will be here to smell it till far too late. They uncoil their burden around the hall corner and out the back door. Katie has lifted one of the half-dozen duplicate keys from her mother's desk—no one noticed in the afternoon's melee, just as she figured—and she locks the door behind them, so that they won't immediately be suspected. The dogwood trees on either side of the door, the oak—now, these she would rather not destroy. She tries to be surreptitious in kicking the rope toward the building rather than near the vegetation. But Sean mutters, "Don't be stupid," and whips her bare leg with the thick twine as he casts it into the middle of the path.

The rocket bombs are set in a row there in the grass where they can't be easily seen, which they might have been next to the bare stucco walls. "Right," she says, squeezing his neck, helping him now so it goes fast, playing out the rope, keeping low, even though they are behind the building with little chance of being seen. There is no night security. Riva is far too simple.

Or is it cheap? They've laughed about this. She could be innocent, or simply unwilling to spend money on locks and night guards. Or maybe she thinks she can create an energy shield like a missile barrier or some other mystical thing. Whatever. She's left herself vulnerable. And Sean keeps saying she deserves what she gets, giving so much less to her own daughter than to—well, to Leeny, to Peggy Lubbock—though she talks so big about light and truth.

This is the night to show her who gets what.

They reach the end of the walkway, scrape the hissing lighter to a frightening height, hold it to the thick end of rope, and run down the stairs to the artificial pond in the back. Katie knows from Riva that all the elements are needed for truly effective energetic events—earth, water, fire, air. Tonight the grass is earth, the pond is water, the fire is coming, and when the sound of air, like a little cry, spirals up from somewhere in the building, her mind runs away from thoughts of who might walk in or what she might be giving up. She forces herself to think only *good, all the elements are in place.*

They crouch on the path near the maze, Sean's hand on her back under her little knit top, following the flame before it hits the rocket bombs one by one and then whooshes into the open door of the building. The air whistles. Sean grabs her wrist and pulls her back further into the hedge, kissing her hard with his tongue, stubble scratching her cheek, calloused finger and dirty thumb pinching her breast, red heat matching violent, upshooting heat.

Everything to Do With You

2003

I. Master healers know

ALL THIS BEGAN, LIKE A FAIRY TALE, WITH THE ARRIVAL
of a stranger—*wizard,* I thought in the flash of rescue, though
he looked like an ordinary fisherman that moment he rose from
the river, waders glistening to the hips and vest hung about
with mysterious feathery flies. I might have screamed—*danger,
intruder!*—if I hadn't already been fully occupied containing
Garrett's amphibious fit, clutching and wheezing and grasping at
limbs. The wanderer could have worn hides or magician's robes
and I'd have been no more able to resist his help, no less grateful
once he'd given it.

He must have heard Garrett thrashing, must have seen me
lurching through the marshy shallows toward the river's edge
where we could administer a rite of redress—an ampule of calm-
ing herbs, usually, that I carried in a pouch like a phylactery. But
we had to get to the shore to use it. Mr. Ordinary Angler took
two or three Puss-'n-Boots strides through the cattails to place
both hands around Garrett's head like a cap, first searching his
face, then gazing off into the scrub oak toward nothing I could
see. He said, "Hmm"—not really a wizard's incantation, is it?—
and flicked his fingers, as if getting rid of a mosquito, before he
replaced them more firmly in Garrett's hair, twisting his wrist as
if Garrett were a jar of fish eggs whose lid wouldn't come off. This
happened more quickly than it takes to say, and ended when, as
if fixing a seal, he gripped the boy's forehead with his palm, then
resolutely pulled it away.

"It's been tough for you." He spoke to both of us, though he looked into Garrett's eyes. "I can't promise, but I bet it feels easier after this. Safer." He smiled widely, not at all naïve about his effect on me—part single-mom *thump-thump-thump*, part deep-down Maynard skepticism, part—where did this come from?—*yes please yes.*

"Oh," he added, hoisting over his shoulder an old rod and reel lying in the juniper at the shoreline, "by the way, this has everything to do with you, you know. Yes—" when I pointed at myself in disbelief, *are you talking to me?*—"you."

He turned on his heel, the dip-and-shrug of his shoulder setting my stomach aflutter, and sauntered off, southward on the trail down to the Lodge.

I swear it happened this way, Garrett's faded tee shirt and blond hair dripping as he stood with me, chest heaving, brow furrowed as he stared after the wizard, puzzled but still. Almost I might have said *calm*. Which was the thing to note: there he stood, his hand on the place where Roland's hand had been, calmly looking after the man—or his echo. Roland was already gone.

"Better," he said.

I looked at him carefully. In fact he did look "better," not wheezing with fear but sound, firmly on dry ground, collected.

If this had been a mere coughing spell, or a one-time trial—if the stranger had crossed our path at midday, or on any other day of the summer but this, or if Garrett had ever responded to prescriptions, therapies, or priesthood blessings—if any of these, the fisherman might have magnetized me less. But no. It was dusk on the eve of the Festival at the end of the summer of grief. Nothing ever helped Garrett's attacks but time and patience. And what, may I ask, was that about it being all my fault? I could hardly let him disappear.

"Wait!" I called, my arms around my boy. "What does that mean?" But he didn't reappear.

WE DID NOT HAVE TIME, HOWEVER, TO PAUSE ON THE SHORE and peruse each other with widened eyes. Cold would descend, and dark, and Garrett had standing plans with his father on Friday evenings. Not to mention this particular weekend's big event, the first-ever Suaros Lodge Arts Festival, designed to divert Adela Suaros from her paralysis of grief. In a strange bid for distraction, Carlos Suaros had booked Annie Macdougal, poet, my own anti-sister and one locus of my many secret ambivalences, to read her work on the Saturday night. Adopted child of my estranged mother Riva (who was, and remained, Adela's good friend), Annie held out hope, Carlos thought, for some kind of rebirth after the mountain's terrible spring. She herself had suggested that for the Festival she should stay with us, with Garrett and me. She envied our solitude, our fine and private place beyond the reach of Lodge clientele. She would be making her way up the trail to the cabin even as we stood there gaping. We must bestir ourselves.

I rubbed the sand from Garrett's hair and—remarkable—he didn't shudder or pull away. He reached for my hand, another first, as we crossed the little rock-strewn expanse between the river and the house to make dinner, dicing carrots and onions on the wide pine table, saying little, pondering calmly what had just happened and by whose hands.

The soup simmered, filling the house with brothy steam, and we'd set out our favorite ceramic bowls and pewter spoons as contemplatively as two thunderstruck people can, before Annie's shadow crossed the doorway. The silhouette of her bulging pack in the low evening sun sprang across the wall like a hunchback crone come to check on the work of the wizard.

But I shook off the impression. This was no hunchback crone. Just Annie—if she could ever be "just Annie."

"Come on!" She turned almost before she entered, dropping her backpack and beckoning us back outside, her eyes bright, thick cinnamony hair pulled back in haphazard *take-me-as-I-am* fashion. "The keynote speaker's my teacher—get ready!"

"Teacher? Professor from the U? Guru?" We all jumped. Practically slamming into her, arriving earlier than expected, Garrett's father danced, his profile prickly on the floormat. When Sean stepped into the dusk-dark kitchen, the new tattoo on his right bicep glowed: CTR. "Choose the Right." How typical—a Mormon children's lyric on a burning man's limb. He said, "How about you, Gare? Ready?"

Annie stepped inside, shaking her jacket off like a version of Red dropping her Riding Hood in the grandmother's vestibule, bantering with the wolf. Sean—parolee out on good behavior, still, to everyone's surprise—turned his grin on her proprietarily. He trout-fished with his son on our river Fridays at dusk, nine months of the year, spring, summer, fall. *Their* time. The outings anchored their two lives so effectively—though for such different reasons—that my saying no would have been worst mischief. I allowed them; Annie made light of them. None of us forgot the offenses linking our pasts.

"Eat first," Garrett said.

Producing the syllables pleased him. So did his father's and Annie's staggers backward in surprise. "Talking, are we?" Sean searched our son's face as the wizard had.

Garrett's hands flew to his eyes, a familiar gesture of invisibility. Then they fluttered back to his sides as if he'd forgotten why. "You, too," he said to Annie.

Two appropriate phrases, one after the other! His father set down his fishing gear next to Annie's pack, took the steps from door to table in two swift paces, and swung the boy up to the ceiling, crowing, "Hey, kiddo! This is good! Isn't this good, Katie-o?"

Don't call me that. I didn't say it aloud. We both knew not to break the spell. "It's good," I said.

We ate, exchanging raised eyebrows across spoonfuls of spicy soup and fragments of information about Annie's part in this year's Festival. Less interested in her New Writer Reading status than in casting for brown trout, Sean tumbled his empty bowl in the sink, scooped up Garrett's reel and tackle box by the wood stove and took Garrett's hand possessively in his own. Garrett butted his shoulder against my hip.

"Have fun," I said. *Watch yourselves,* I meant. Garrett nodded—I didn't need to tell him. His attacks, his father's moods—two things they'd both learned to be wary of. Then they were gone, back to the river to cast flies.

Annie and I, for our part, tossed our own dishes, threw on jackets, and jogged the mile-long trail through fallen aspen and tall wildflowers across the streambed. Deliberately we turned our heads away from the slope rising sharply east of us where acres of pine lay flattened and scattered like a child's game of sticks, saying nothing of avalanche or snowmobile or Logan Suaros's bones below.

Instead we looked forward. Lights flickered through the aspen from the back of the lodge. Fountains burbled, their water pumped from the river. The double back doors of the conference room slid open like the entrance to a magic cave, an extension of our natural evening-lit path, reached by a set of low-rising stairs made of stone pastel as dusk. Annie bounded effortlessly in. I followed, slower.

The auditorium held fifty or sixty. Only a few gray-padded folding chairs sat empty at the top of a sloping set of removable tiers, every other seat already filled. Carlos Suaros, owner of the Lodge and of the cabin where I lived, stepped to the dais. A handsome, kind man, solid (not fat, as my father always pointed out in his defense), his second-generation latinity showing up in his name and his faint accent, his authority in this crowd came not merely from his mass or his role as the lodge's owner. His intelligent good nature invited loyalty. And then there was his wife, the competent Adela, university-educated and active Mormon, angel to everyone, local herb woman and primary author—everyone knew it—of the Lodge's ultimate success, though she always gave credit to Carlos. Her despair this past six months disabled us all.

Flashing gray eyes at us now from under his Stetson, cheeks twitching with the responsibility of being host, Carlos raised his arms. Applause swelled while those of us still standing draped our wraps on chair backs, seated ourselves, and turned our focus forward.

The room hushed.

"Tonight is the first night of our first annual Festival," he reminded us, pulling us with his crisped t's into the enchanted circle of *festival*. "You'll hear from our keynote speaker now. Tomorrow he leads a class, after which our very own poet will read her work, inspired by him." The whoop of applause for Annie surprised me, but she waved, unabashed, at the faces turning to find her.

"Now," said Carlos when they'd turned back to him, "allow me to present our guest and workshop leader for the weekend." Half the audience leaped to their feet, whistling and clapping. "He's famous the world over, if this crowd's any indication." We could barely hear him over the din. "You're already welcoming him, so I give to you Roland Alder, master healer from the coast of California."

I hadn't known his name earlier, of course, and he wasn't in fishing garb any more. A mauve silk shirt opened to the third shell button, and his sharply creased navy slacks revealed the toes of deerskin moccasins. But that's who it was, stepping from behind the rostrum to stand at Carlos's side—Annie's teacher, the fisherman wizard.

It was a full minute before the room was quiet enough for Roland to speak. In that suspended moment, his eyes caught mine as if I'd called his name. Did anyone notice how we studied each other? Oh, he remembered me as clearly as I did him. But he did more. Checking in with some cosmic search engine, he accessed my file, probed my character, saw my life, knew my purpose. I stood exposed, astonished. Finally, he nodded—*ah yes. You.* Then he began his talk.

"I'm not used to giving speeches." His voice was the same one—surprisingly youthful, though deep and kind—that had assured my son and me we'd be better from now on. "I demonstrate through you, yourselves, what I have learned is true. Which is this: you co-create your life. There is no downstream. Your choices jar your neighbor, her actions impact you, and both of you fibrillate the universe." He waited for the laughter to subside. "No, really! For proof, look to your symbol body! Every part of you—tissues, fluids, nerves, desires—resonates harmoniously, or not, with everything in your field, and everyone else's field as well. In fact, if everything is conscious, then literally and figuratively, you embody God."

I'd been tutored in the energetics of flowers, harmonics of herbs, essence of healing in human touch—Riva, my mother, and Adela, her friend and mine, taught me these from childhood. Also, my father's God was literal flesh and blood, embodiment indeed, according to the doctrine. But I kept a private shard of uncertainty. None of it had helped my son. I believed only that Gare's sufferings paid his father's and my sins. Not resonance but justice ruled this earth, apportioned with exactness by a law-abiding God.

Yet Roland had lifted our burden in a trice.

(*Perhaps.* His last remark still echoed).

Now he penetrated the risers, touching someone's bicep, someone else's forehead. He gestured toward a woman hunkered in her chair a few rows below us, her neck immobilized by a metal and plastic brace. Her colorless hair draggled over the apparatus in listless hanks. She looked up at him, bleak. I felt for a moment as if I saw her through a darkened glass, a flash of memory …

"Nobody talked to you about what you find to be a pain in the neck, I'll bet. Did they?" He blinked when everybody laughed. "I don't joke. Nobody made the connection between your injury and your life. I'd bet my life on it. Can you come to the end of the row without discomfort—?" He swept his arm toward an empty seat in the aisle. She put her hands up to her face, a sort of clawed version of Garrett's gesture of invisibility.

"Go on, do it," someone said—a woman to her left, who seemed to be with her in dress and attitude, though healthier in all respects. Sighing, the woman in the brace detached herself from her seat, yanking her skirt from where it caught. We heard it tear, saw her stand shocked for a moment, the fringe of the fabric dangling. She bit at a thumbnail as she sidled across two or three others in the row toward Roland, her shoes squeaking unevenly as if she reconsidered every step, making her way blindly through a maze.

Roland gestured to the empty seat at the end of the row. She slid into it.

"With your permission?"

So gently we almost didn't see it happen, Roland put his hands around her head. At his touch, her posture changed, as if in giving her head to Roland she suddenly grew roots and drank from the earth. I imagined his hands warm, dry, strong, like the hands of my father and his friends when they blessed me with the gift of the Holy Ghost after I was baptized, when I was eight. Solid, comforting, secure.

Funny—I hadn't thought of that in years.

But now, between those palms, Roland turned her head a millimeter to the left, a micromeasurement to the right, to show its range of motion, stinted and severe.

He caressed her left shoulder. "Your daughter—your sister?—your mother? Ancient sadness. Generations of women." Stroking her right shoulder, he murmured, "And some male who has authority over you—ah, not sadness. Much less neutral. Hmm?"

Her eyes closed. Her body swayed. "Our *something*," she started to say, but on the third syllable her voice rose to a near-hysterical pitch, rising to a keening like a kite on a loosened string. She caught at him with desperate fingers. He steadied himself, making himself an anchor until he gave in and became the kite, his energy rising with hers out the window, up to the heavens, though he bent to her with his arms around her. If I could trust my thumping heart, every soul in the room leaned toward that embrace like leaves to the sun.

The woman howled into his neck for a week.

It was only a minute or so, really, before she pushed him away. Wiping her nose on her jacket sleeve, she sniffed. "Awkward. I'm sorry."

"Sorry isn't appropriate," he said, so kindly I thought she (or I) might faint. He kept one hand on the back of her neck. (*Me, too! Me, too!* Which of us wasn't yearning for this from our places?)

Annie had the presence of mind to scramble down the aisle with a tissue. Roland handed it to the woman, who blew loudly. "Do you want to heal the pain for good?" he asked curiously, wiping his own eyes with his free thumb. "Or did you just need to know I feel it too?"

"Never … heal for good."

Roland kissed the top of her head. Then he addressed her companion, younger than she but older than when—yes—I'd seen her last, seven years ago. She'd scrutinized the little tableau tonight from her seat further in the row.

"This is a mutual suffering?" he said, taking in the whole room yet questioning only them. From their separate patches of grief, each nodded. Roland beckoned and the younger woman inched across the intervening audience members. Stronger than her sister-wife, she seemed, her eyes a straightforward blue, her still-supple brown braid swinging as she came decisively to Roland. When she was within reach, Roland took her hands as if they were precious and joined them to the other's.

"If you'll allow me—?" Again, each nodded, one timid, the other precise.

Roland laid one hand over the seated woman's sternum. In a gesture both intimate and respectful, he slid the other just inside the back of her brace. I could see her relax into his hands, trusting. As with Garrett this afternoon, he closed his eyes, listening for something the rest of us couldn't hear. He said mildly, "Maybe if you forgive him."

The woman's head snapped back as much as it could in its pinions. "Who?"

He had an answer: "*You* know. That's all that matters. Shift the vibration—check in with yourself, ask who and how. Watch—then everything will shift."

A moment passed. Two. Then, as if a signal had been given or a latch lifted, the woman's head turned, slowly but inexorably under Roland's hands, all the way to the right within its collar, toward Roland, and then all the way left. At the furthest points she winced. A rippling "ahhh" rose in the hall. The standing sister covered her face with one hand.

"You'll find this hurts less now," Roland said, removing first one hand then the other, one finger at a time, as if drawing them out of molasses. "Don't take the brace off yet. When you've held on to—this—so many months, strength to change must build up slowly. But I promise, you won't need it too much longer. Get help during tomorrow's workshop, now. You have each other, yes?"

"Yes," said the younger woman fiercely. "We have each other."

So they still did. I ducked my head: *please don't let them see me and remember.*

AFTER THE PRESENTATION, AFTER FRIENDS AND STUDENTS and devotees had flocked to Roland and wished him well and touched his hands and funneled slowly out the carved front doors, Annie and I stayed behind so she could introduce us properly. "We've met," he said, taking my hand judiciously. "How's your—son, is he?"

"Good, I think," I said. "I need to ask you—"

"I'm tired tonight, if you don't mind." A statement of fact, not avoidance or unkindness. "I do better on a good night's sleep. Perhaps we'll talk tomorrow, hmm? After Annie's reading? All of us?" He waved his arm, including Carlos and Adela, Annie and me. He squeezed my hand and let it go, kissed Annie's cheek, and turned away to join his hosts, who were waiting to usher him to his quarters. We were left to trudge the steep way back up the moonlit trail.

"Why didn't you tell me you knew him?"

"I didn't have a chance," I said. "The question is, how do *you* know him?"

"Riva introduced us—she met him through your aunt. Suzanne? The one in California? They've always kept in touch."

Oh.

But that wasn't all. "Riva'll try to make it here tomorrow to hear me read."

So Roland knew my mother, drew her here. It shouldn't have surprised me. They were the same age (I could see that now) and had (even easier to perceive) the same energetic mold. Still, it complicated things. Was nothing I wanted to hear.

At the cabin, Garrett lay on the sofa in the main room, shining, I thought, in his sleep. Sean was absent. That wasn't unusual. He often dropped Garrett off with a wave and nod. But tonight all of a sudden I wanted them together, present and awake, evidence of my past, keys to a possible future—right here in the walls of my home.

WHAT'S "HEALING"? MAYBE YOU THINK HEALING IS A *matter of identifying, obtaining, and imbibing your substance of choice. No, friends, thanks for the laughs, but you all know that's not healing. So what is? A few sessions with a good shrink? A personal trainer and a nutritional specialist? A surgeon who can replace a part that doesn't work any more, whether it's an arm or an eye or a heart?*

You go to a helper of any kind—a doctor, a shrink, a miracle worker, I don't care what you call it—you go to a helper because you want change, you want transformation, and you believe you can't do it alone. If you could have by now, you would have.

So you go for help, right? And what happens nowadays if you go to the doc is that he, or she, looks at you through a scope. Uses an instrument of some kind. Pokes you, taps you, consults a book. Keeps you at a distance. If anybody touches you with their hands in a doctor's office or a hospital, it's a nurse. And oh, boy, if anyone tunes in to the entirety of you, including your physical structure, your emotional body, your mental constructs, your energy field, and your karma—well, that's a rare and unusual accident.

Let me ask you a question. How many doctors, how many people of any profession or persuasion do you know who equate 'physical healing' with collective, multi-dimensional, universal responsibility? How many perceive that not only yours but their past choices are part of the present situation?

I LAY DOWN FULLY DRESSED ON MY OWN BED, SLEPT, AND dreamed. At the head of an unfamiliar path lined with wildflowers in colors and shapes waking life had never seen, Roland stood poised beside me, his hand a tingling intensity at the small of my back, enabling me to see Garrett farther down the flowered lane, leading his father toward us. Behind them? Only darkness, and a tiny point of fire.

Suddenly, Annie shook my shoulder harshly. "Katie, get up. Carlos is here— it's bad news— Sean—they found him bleeding and unconscious down at the Lodge by his truck. They've called an ambulance. I'll stay here with Garrett. Carlos will take you down."

II. The thing you're most afraid of, what you'd banish if you could

MY CABIN, FOR ALL ITS SOLITUDE, COULD BE REACHED two ways. You could take the footpath from the Lodge or you could drive up Old State Road 36, a steep meander of gravel and dirt that paralleled the river on the side opposite us, closed in the winter and early spring, with multiple rest stops by the water for fishermen's and families' use in the summer and fall. To get to my place from the road, you had to cross the water, as Roland had done yesterday, and though it was relatively shallow this time of year, if you didn't find the ruins of the one-lane footbridge a couple of hundred yards above the cabin, you might be discouraged from making the passage.

The avalanche that killed Logan sent a force of wind that collapsed the ancient bridge. While machines and dogs and rescue squads picked through tons of snow and rocks west of us, Garrett and I strapped on our snowshoes, thinking maybe we'd find a miracle. Instead, the searchers found Logan crushed under half a mountain of debris, and we found a crumble of timber where the week before had been beams and a walkway. Losing Logan collapsed Adela nearly beyond repair. We were broken, too. The loss of the bridge was nothing.

Ordinarily, I hiked everywhere. If I needed winter transportation, I snowshoed—I had nothing but time and my boy on my hands, after all—but there were other methods available to me if I needed them. Now the pop-*pop*-pop of the Suaros' ancient Honda XL 200 bike's engine outside, once Annie drew my attention to it, was as sharp an alarm as a siren. It took us ten or twelve jarring minutes down the canyon, bouncing over breaks and bumps barely noticed on foot, drawn by vexing forces through moonlit sage and aspen to the asphalt parking lot. An ambulance's red light spiraled, its engine stuttering reproachfully. Carlos rammed the kickstand down.

"Head trauma, possibly," someone said. Paramedics passed papers among themselves and over to me. "Coma."

"You'd better call your father." Carlos tossed the Lodge's up-to-the-minute mobile phone at me as I climbed into the van. I held myself steady, one arm braced against each wall of the ambulance's interior as, flashing its light, it hugged the tight curves down the canyon to the small hospital in town.

"What happened?" I asked the EMT, but he had to watch the snaking road and didn't answer. Sean himself, yellow-faced, his head flattened into the gurney like an exotic image of death, gave no sign of awareness.

I punched into Carlos's device the number that would ring whether its owner was in Salt Lake City or at his ten-room "cabin" in the mountains of northern Idaho five hundred miles away. "Dad," I said when Paul Maynard barked "Hello."

"Katie? Where are you?"

"Something's happened," I said.

"You never call unless it has," he reminded me, "and never at this time of night. Or morning. Is Garrett bad again?"

"Ah," I said, "no, actually, Garrett's better than he's been in a long time. Sean," I said it quickly. "Sean this time." I told him the little I knew.

"Ah, Katie." His sigh evoked disappointments still reverberating through our lives. "I suppose they'll need me there." He was the convict's sponsor. "Anything immediate you want?" I said no. "Keep me posted. I'll be there as soon as I can." We hung up.

Carlos's truck sped behind us into the silent center of town, past the family-friendly grocer and retail in the main square, and out, rolling to the glaring Emergency Room sign outside the cinder-block hospital. I let myself onto the blacktop. Carlos tucked my hand into the crook of his arm, hurrying with me behind the paramedics through automatic sliding doors.

I signed forms. Attendants trundled Sean through another set of doors into the dark innards of the building. The wheels of the system set spinning in other rooms, Carlos and I were left alone together in the waiting room to—well—wait.

"What happened?" I took the Coke he plucked for me from a machine. "How—?"

"I don't know, Katie-girl," he said, his voice tired. "We were all inside, you know."

"Don't you have people to make sure something like this doesn't happen?"

He shook his head, amazed. "Never needed them."

An attendant in scrubs stepped through the sliding doors with a clipboard. "Katie Maynard? You're the patient's next of kin?"

"We have a son," I said. "Not married."

"I see," the young man said, writing something down in the notes fastened to his clipboard. "Dr. Vistaunet will be out in just a minute—oh, here he is. Dr. V? This is the patient's ex-wife."

"No," I said. "Remember me, Dr. Vistaunet?" I reached over to shake his hand, a long-fingered limb I hadn't pumped since I learned to handle Garrett's attacks despite this man's prescriptions. I'd almost forgotten him. Now his face—thinner than I remembered, lined, framed by neat gray hair at alpine height—furrowed for a moment. Then his eyes cleared. "Oh, yes, the autistic child," he said.

"Not autistic."

He hesitated for the barest length of time. "Well, you've got another difficulty on your hands now," he said. In his voice was neither judgment nor kindness. "Your—husband's—still unconscious. No response at all. We can't pinpoint a cause—he's bleeding from the ear, the only external sign. Has anything like this happened before?"

"Not to him." Dr. Vistaunet knew Garrett's history, though.

"Do you know what happened?"

"Less than you."

"Have a theory?"

"None whatsoever." Except that Garrett had been touched by a healer this afternoon, and it had everything to do with me.

Again he hesitated. "Well, cardiovascular and pulmonary systems are stabilized. You'll want a brain scan as soon as possible."

"Maybe someone will," I said, feeling hope recede, like slipping below deep water.

"Any idea what the prognosis might be?" Carlos asked from behind me.

"Best case scenario, he wakes within the hour. If he does, we observe him—can he see? Speak? Remember who he is? That'll give us data to work with. But first he has to wake up."

"In the meantime?"

Dr. Vistaunet looked suddenly vulnerable. "Worst case scenario," he said, "I'm sorry to tell you, he's completely disabled. Unable to communicate. Amnesic." I took that in. "But don't anticipate. Every brain is different. He may recover fully. You never know. It would help if we knew the cause."

"What do we do?" I asked.

"Go home," he said wearily. "I'm going to." He pointed me to the admittance window on the other side of the door. His coat swished as he turned away. I gave the nail-filing receptionist Carlos's mobile number and my father's, and pulled on my jacket, suddenly impelled to flee that waiting room, faintly lit now by first hints of summer dawn.

But Carlos said, "I'd like to see him. You can stay here. I'll be quick."

He was halfway across the room before I realized I was going too. I leaped behind him into the pale green elevator, smelling of antiseptic, just deep enough for a gurney and its occupant. He pressed the button for the second floor.

"I hate hospitals," Carlos said as the car creaked skyward. "There's nothing healing about them. Has Adela told you how much time we spent in hospitals with Logan when he was little? For asthma. One of the reasons we came up here." He grimaced. "Much good it did us."

The elevator door ground open. The pregnant teenager at the nurses' station blinked at her computer and told us Sean's room number, "Two-twenty-five" (I wouldn't forget—the two of us were twenty-five now, all those years between us), pointed down the hall to her left, and clicked the machine back to the Solitaire game we'd interrupted. We moved past two closed doors and slipped into the narrow private room where Sean lay, his head bandaged, an IV in his arm, his body deflated under a beige throw, the monitor's beep a steady grounding. Carlos moved around to the top of the bed, peering intently at Sean's disheveled head.

A young intern poked into the doorway. "Just doing rounds," he said. "What are you folks up to? A blessing?"

Carlos's head came up. If a family member didn't show up in this small town with a phial of consecrated oil to administer priesthood blessings to a newly-admitted patient, the Mormon doctors did it themselves, affirming to spouses and parents the deepseated certainty that if the spiritual body were addressed, the physical would surely thrive.

"No," I said quickly. "We'll be out in a minute."

The intern waved his clipboard—*whatever you like*—and disappeared from view.

"I'd be happy to bless him," Carlos said.

"Sean would hate it."

"Come help me," Carlos said. "Let's just put our hands here. You can pray."

I swatted his suggestion away. "Women don't give blessings."

"If you don't want to, at least let me."

"Carlos, I don't think—" Blessings were for the pure in heart, the meek of spirit. Everything Sean had never been.

But Carlos cocked his head until I said, "Oh, just do it!"

He turned to Sean, his hands seeking a place to hold and bless, listening, his palms finally gentle against Sean's temples. Low-voiced, he uttered words of comfort over Sean's indifferent head.

HE AND THE CHILD FOLLOWED THE OLD ROUTINE: FIND THE right spot on the bank, the deep pool below, the riffle of fishtails at dusk, watching always to be sure the child was settled, safe, well, his eyes aware, his focus clear. Choose the perfect flies, painstakingly made at the father's bare table in the evenings after work. Then cast. Position the head. Cock the wrist. Follow through with the forearm poised.

But tonight, his father saw, the boy was different. His eyes didn't squint or jitter, didn't scurry from what they beheld. He smelled different too, not so much like a frightened babe but like a child at the edge of a new-dug well, damp earth and cool water and a ladle poised to plumb its depths.

The child said, "Jesus came."

His father said, "Jesus?"

The boy mimed the vest, his thumbs twisting the flies hooked into the Velcro. "Fishing." Patting the top of his own head, he said, "Better."

The child settled his line over water, let it sit for a reasonable length of time, considered the space behind and above him before he cast again.

Curious.

"Yes," said his father. "Better. That seems to be true."

He'd have to ask the boy's mother. Sometimes he was certain she knew things he did not—might sometime invite him to learn. When he thought this, he saw a door opening—not her cabin door but an invisible thickening she wove in the air between him and her-and-the-boy, a barrier he couldn't disperse. Lately his urge to fight through it was as strong as the urge for sex.

Ah, it was too hard. They'd never been truly together, he and the mother of the boy. He wanted her to see how changed they both were. If only he could make his way through to her—could perhaps ask about the Jesus who blessed their son. Maybe it would be the beginning of something whose end would be that she'd let him come live with them in their cabin. They could be a family. They could start again, remake the thing so badly misbegotten.

"WE HAVE TO ASK GARRETT," CARLOS SAID AT LAST. "HE was the last person with him. What happened while they fished?"

"I have no idea," I said.

Always mindful, Carlos asked if I'd told Garrett yet, and whether he'd have an attack if I did.

"I don't think we have to worry about that," I said. "Roland healed him."

Carlos took that in, his dark eyebrows high. "You believe Garrett's cured and you won't let the priesthood bless Sean?"

The wakeful intern came around the door again. "Dr. V says go home," he said kindly. "We'll call if there's a change."

When we walked into the Lodge a half hour later, Adela met us in the hall, sleepy and soft, pulling the sash of her terry-cloth robe tight. "What are you doing here?" Slowly, she turned indignant.

"Grabbing the scooter so Katie can sleep in her own bed," Carlos said.

"No, you aren't," she said. "That boy may be in a coma, but he can feel and hear. What if he wakes up? Someone should be there!"

"Oh, Dell," Carlos said. "Katie's exhausted."

"You're the obvious one," she said to me, ignoring her husband. "The doctor said to leave. He said there's nothing we can do." I sounded heartless even to myself.

Adela, herbalist and healer in her own right, counted off on her fingers the things an unconscious man's family could do— tell him his story, sing his song, hold his hand. Be there. Finally, she pursed her lips and said she'd go herself. She gathered me into a sympathetic hug, but I knew I'd been chastised. "Take Garrett to Roland's workshop. He's—well, you saw what he did with the Lubbocks."

So she recognized the sister-wives, too, the woman with the neck brace and her companion, though it had been seven years since the catastrophe that bound us.

"What *did* Roland do?" I asked her quickly, while she still held me close. She would know. "Is Peggy Lubbock really well? Would a doctor take off her brace?"

She smoothed my hair. "You sound like your father. You saw, didn't you?"

"You said he healed Garrett, too," Carlos reminded me.

"*What?*"

"He came out of the water with Garrett in the middle of a fit. Put his hands on him and made it stop."

"When?"

"This—yesterday—afternoon. That's what I want to know— who knows how long it'll last?"

"That's not what you said at the hospital," Carlos reminded me, not ungently.

"Oh, Katie!" Adela made little fists and shook them triumphantly. "This is wonderful news!"

"How do you *know*?" I heard my own voice shearing off toward doubt, or worse than doubt.

"I know," she said firmly. "And so do you. Here's what I say: you go to Roland's workshop in the morning, and I'll stay with Sean. Then if you can, bring Roland to the hospital at lunch."

"Right," said Carlos, ever the supportive husband. "That's what we'll do."

I MIGHT AS WELL HAVE STAYED WITH SEAN. FOR THE BRIEF time before dawn, I did nothing but wind my sheets around me noisily, turning from fetal to outstretched side to back, arms out-flung in vain attempts to banish rising and falling images. Sean bandage-swathed in his hospital bed. My son, calm and normal. The healer's hands on Peggy Lubbock's shoulders. Finally, I threw the bedcover to the floor and sat on the edge of the mattress, running my fingers through my hair and scowling as if I could frighten into silence the dippers and grouse whose calls announced the sun. Before either of my housemates stirred, I slid on a pair of flip-flops and went outside in my cotton nightshirt, down the path to the strand.

The river's movement was muted in the low light, waiting for sun to call it into full vigor. I let the chilly ripples lap my feet, forcing me to full consciousness. Dippers skittered across the water with a high *zit, zit* before they dove. Millions of dimpled aspen leaves above and behind me chattered a rumor of autumn. Light filtered between the near peaks, igniting the water's surface, spot-and-dapple. What happened here yesterday afternoon? What happened here last night? What were the Lubbocks doing here, why must I encounter Riva? What synchronicity placed those women like the Furies in my way and unmanned Sean the very night they came?

"I'M AFRAID OF THE WATER," THE GIRL-CHILD SAYS AT THE EDGE of the lake. Worse since her mother's defection, in absence of anchor or air or earth, she's loath to go where gravity wavers, where light or oxygen aren't. At baptism she clenched her teeth, immersion no less risky for redemption at its other end. Airplanes, horses, boats: she aborts all offers, no gambling with peril, select another mode if possible, say no if not. She chooses every time the sheltered site, the task low to ground, the cleared path. The lake, she's sure, is death, the river dominion of demons.

I nearly dove in, detonated, when my father touched me on the shoulder.

III. Not only your past choices make today, but theirs ...

"KATIE," PAUL SAID AT MY LEAP AND STRANGLED CRY. "IT'S just me."

I scrambled, smoothing my hair, arranging my shirt, pretending control by asking questions: Had he come up the trail on foot, or had I not heard the bike? And before that, how long driving? Sean—had he seen him? My father's barely rumpled clothes (pale yellow Polo shirt, dew-hemmed Levis) gave nothing away. He wasn't all that tall. His shoulders weren't broad, and his hair thinned further every year. But he was trim and fit, and he carried himself like a self-made executive, used to hard work and responsibility, and here he was, with me by the river.

"Not yet," he said now, about having been to the hospital. "I came straight here. Of course."

"Of course," I said. "What's next?"

"We find out what happened, who did what. And we do whatever we must. Of course."

For the first time since Annie shook my shoulder, I breathed a sigh of relief.

BACK AT THE CABIN I FIXED TOAST AND BOYSENBERRY JAM and cups of morning tea for my father and my son, who was dressing himself when we slipped in the door. Annie, who had waited for me to return, nodded to my father and slipped away to the workshop's setting-up. I tried to gauge: were Garrett's movements smoother, more coherent? When he threw on his hooded sweatshirt, greeted his grandfather (with no more words than usual), and gulped his tea—was it easier? We had no effort-meter, but at least there were no flurries, no single hint of fit. Then Paul asked:

"Garrett, son, last night—"

My boy didn't hesitate: "Fish!" He pulled open the refrigerator door and pointed: three fresh browns in plastic wrap, cleaned and ready to pan-fry.

I squatted beside him, holding him around the waist with my right arm, smelling the river on his face and hair. "Kiddo," I said. "Your dad? Something happened when he went down to the Lodge. He got hurt." Garrett inhaled sharply, his hands to his eyes. I sucked my breath in, steeled for an attack that didn't come.

"Where?"

"On his head," I said. He shook himself and repeated the question. Not where was his father's injury—where did it happen?

"I don't know, buddy—we wondered if you did."

"Did anyone come by while you were fishing?" Paul stooped to Garrett's level as I stood. "Did your dad do or say anything different than he usually does?"

Garrett bent his head, studying the floor. "Jesus," he said. That was it.

Which reminded me. I stood, held out my hand. "Want to see your friend from yesterday?"

His eyes lit up. "Jesus!"

Now he wanted to hurry. We threw on jackets and headed down the trail, puffing in the cool-to-warming morning air. I pointed out the bike tracks.

"That's Carlos," I said. "I rode to the hospital with him."

"Jesus fix," Garrett said, running ahead.

"He could," my father said, matter-of-fact in his faith.

"Carlos gave him a blessing even though I said no. But Garrett means somebody else." I told him about Roland.

He harrumphed. "You think a charlatan can heal your boy, but you won't bless his father?"

I studied him in surprise, stopping for a moment in our progress down. "*I* couldn't," I said. "Women don't."

He shrugged, bewildered at his own slip. "That wasn't what I meant."

"Well, Carlos did bless Sean. In the end I didn't stop him. And Roland—well, Adela doesn't think he's a fake."

"What do you think?"

I shrugged. I didn't want to tell him what the healer said about my part in the matter.

NOBODY BUT ROLAND NOTICED AS WE TIPTOED IN THE side door of the Lodge's conference room, found a small stack of gray metal chairs folded against the wall, and set up three for ourselves at the back of the room so we could observe without taking part. A smaller crowd than had been there last night sat or lay on cushions spread around the room, now bare of chairs except for ours. Annie and the Lubbock women occupied opposite corners, a score or so of last night's participants taking up the space between. A long table had been pushed against the east wall, draped in hunter green and set with a hot water machine, coffee packets and cocoa mix, cups, and a platter of croissants. Roland had changed into gray slacks and a maroon jacquard shirt, more casual than last night's. His hair, still wet from a shower, sprung from his head in dark tendrils. He'd been giving instructions. His students were meditating deeply, locating a life-changing wish.

GO INSIDE. HOW CAN I FIND YOU IF YOU DON'T GO *inside? Don't forget to breathe. It won't help anything if you forget to breathe. Bring to mind, taking all the time you need, the one wish which, if you could have it, you believe your life would be far more to your liking. If nothing comes to mind, call up the one thing you're most afraid of, what you'd banish if you could. Don't decide too quickly. Your body will let you know you've chosen right.*

SUCH ABSORPTION! SUCH DELIBERATION, SUCH SINGLE-mindedness on hopes or fears! Throughout the room, lips puckered in concentration. Heads bowed intently. Shoulders shook. Paul and I waited in our corner, dubious and severe, to see what Roland planned to do with this orgy of navel-gazing.

What he did was wait. Give them space. And come directly to us, the only ones with our eyes open.

Garrett inched closer to me, tucking his shoulder into my armpit. I rested my chin on the top of his head, gently, while I observed with a sort of inner eye the bubble of desire stretch upward and outward to tap all the seams and corners of the room. My boy dug himself into me, his shoulder driving into my ribs (*yes, child, you are my fervent wish*). I could smell the soap he'd washed with this morning, faintly citrus above the sagey tang of the clothes he'd worn down the trail. I glanced over at Annie, apparently inside her own little shroud of lack (what lack was that, I wondered), among her friends in the middle of the room. Still the yearning rose, expanded, and reached a certain equilibrium, like high tide.

The wizard, with us now, held out his hand to my father.

"Roland Alder," he said very quietly. On some other level he still maintained the students' trance, oversaw their inner process. "I don't believe I know you."

"No, you don't," my father said. He kept his arms crossed. "Paul Maynard. Katie's father."

"Ah," said Roland. "It's good you're here. She's making up lost time this weekend. Needs your help."

"What's this?" Paul leaned his chair back against the wall, the better to see Roland.

"You know more than I, I'd guess," Roland said. "But I'll help where I can." He pulled his shoulders back, opening his chest, a display of strength. My father nodded, accepting the offer even if he didn't know quite what it was.

Roland laid a hand on my boy's head. "How are you, young man?"

Garrett put his own hand over Roland's, easy as pie. "Daddy hurt."

The healer knelt to a six-year-old level. "What happened?"

Garrett puzzled over it.

The wizard put his face close. "Tell me, if you can. Show me how to help."

"Jesus," Garrett said, laying his index finger on Roland's forehead.

Roland grasped my son's finger, denying the appellation but acknowledging Garrett's trust. Then he turned to me, searching my face, a curious expression on his own. "Give it a chance," he said, grasping my upper arm. "Don't abdicate now."

"What does that mean?" (Maybe he'd answer this time.)

"When I've had my hands on a person there are things I know. That's all. Have some faith."

My father laughed harshly, thinking, I was sure, of the years of rebellion against God, against faith, that had torn our family apart. "Joke's on you," he said, letting his chair legs down so he could survey the little groups of meditating devotees on the floor in their various inward states. He pointed out the Lubbocks.

"I'm surprised to see them here," he murmured to Roland. "They're volatile, those polygs."

"They have needs too," Roland said mildly. "Remember, nothing's not attached." He stood, offering his hand again to my father, who took it this time. "I'd better move the process on. Please stay—maybe we can do something about that stomach of yours."

My father tried not to register shock. "He likes surprise, doesn't he?"

I nodded. "One of the reasons I like him," I said, realizing it.

I INCHED WITH GARRETT TOWARD THE CENTER OF THE room, curious to discover how in Roland's world wishes were fulfilled. The healer gave instructions. People stirred and spoke in twos and threes so private and so long-winded that my father finally leaned over to ask whether I'd mind if he left to talk to Carlos. He'd retrieve us at the break. I nodded, focused on Roland, and in my peripheral vision I saw one of the double front doors creep open one inch, two. Riva peeked through—my long-separated mother, observing the students in their groups, holding the heavy door ajar for a nanosecond before she noticed us.

At the school, those years ago, people knew immediately I was hers. They said we could have been sisters, twins. I resisted, pointing to the lighter brown of her hair, her more graceful body, the differences in our features. Paul showed up too clearly in my ski-jump nose and straighter frame. I didn't want to see my oval face, my healthy skin or naturally arched eyebrows as evidence of Riva; they were accidents, fortune's fall, I wanted to believe. I hadn't seen her since Garrett was five and a candidate for enrollment in her rebuilt energy school, well-known now in the city below for its success with troubled cases. When I turned aside her offer, choosing my father's and the Suaros' instead (the cabin, the mountain, a life apart), she retreated as if for good—as if she hadn't left for good twenty years before. Now, though, she presented—before I could defend against it, the impression flashed—a mirror of myself, another me, searching through the room for an unidentifiable something whose real nature she meticulously hid.

A something not us. When she saw Paul, about to leave us through the side door, her face wrinkled with confusion. Letting the big oak door fall shut softly, she stepped inside, still roving the room with her eyes. Roland turned to find who'd come. Paul waited, half inside the sliding doorway, half out.

"Finish sharing," Roland said. "Let's gather in the center." While his students came awake, Roland sprang to draw Riva into his arms. He said something low and urgent in her ear; she shook her head, and when she pulled away from his embrace, her hair was tousled, her face pink. Beside us, Paul, making a loud "tch" with his tongue, pushed the sliding side door wide enough to pass through. He shook his head at me (*this is impossible*) as he pulled the door shut behind him and took off down the hall.

"Before we go on," Roland said, "please greet this fine healer and educator!" He raised Riva's arm by their joined hands as if she'd won a much-sought prize (which all his students knew she had, if he spoke of her so highly). "And lucky Annie—this is her spiritual mom—our spiritual parents, you know, being as important as biological ones."

I clenched a fist, forgetting Garrett's hand in my palm. He pulled away. "Mom! Ow!"

"We've been talking about wishes," Roland told Riva by way of reminding his students where they should be in their process. "Our own, but also our place in our partners'. Will you join us?"

Riva looked our way, almost as if asking our permission, almost against her will. She registered Paul's absence. Roland registered the connection between her and me by sight in the same instant. Beckoning, he said, "Come down here, Katie. Find willingness to work with Riva, will you? I promise it will make a difference. One you'll like."

Who could refuse? I went, though my heart festered.

WE ARE ALL ALWAYS OPERATING ON MANY LEVELS AT *once. The physical body agrees to emotions, thoughts fraction- ate against surroundings, the past hums in the genes which have shaped the frame. Talk, talk, talk—that's what you've done so far today, fashioning desires into mental constructs so your partners can understand. Language—like everything on earth—both loosens and binds the truth. Now forget everything*

that's been said in your groups and measure by energy: why do
you lack what you want? What one thing could you change?
What must you and your partner trade so that both of you earn
your desire?

There's no need to name it aloud. Let it form energetically
between your palms, before your heart. Give it time. Earth is
all about time. Remember: the obstacle to perfect happiness
is everyone's free will. But you want it that way, because then
your own free will is assured. This is about finding a way for
all to have free will and joy at the same time. The object is to
discover how you can arrange yourself so your partner has her
wish and so do you.

"WHERE'S NINA?" WE SAT CROSS-LEGGED ON CUSHIONS
facing each other, troubled and uncomfortable. I held Garrett
on my lap, a shield over my vulnerable foreparts.

"Not here. We're—having difficulties." She tightened her lips.

"You must know your wish, then."

She bowed her head in assent. "And yours?"

"Dad," said Garrett quickly. "Fish."

"I heard about that," Riva said, the awkwardness sidestepped
for a moment. "Carlos told me."

"Adela's with Sean now, did he tell you that?"

She nodded. "Maybe you know your wish too." She didn't
wait for response, but closed her eyes. I closed mine too. Prayer?
Energetic resonance? Did the name matter?

What I wanted was—what I wanted was—what I must give up—

How strange, that Riva and I sat here together.

How strange.

In the close silence, I heard my mother murmur, finding her
way with the thread of speech through the maze of what she
lacked.

"Nothing is simple, is it? If I said I always wanted you, you'd
laugh, wouldn't you?" She meant Nina, her mysteriously not-here

Nina. Or did she? "You'd say it had nothing to do with you. It was always me. But—darling—is that fair? I know nothing's fair when everyone has free will. Everyone makes the best choice they can at the time. We could have been so lucky—"

My arms tightened around Garrett. I would never do what she had done. It *was* always her choice to let me go. How dare she? And what in my life, what on this mountain that I loved, would Roland say I must give up for her to have what she lacked? I would never give him up. Never.

"DELA JUST CALLED," CARLOS SAID. HE AND PAUL STOOD AT the double doors with Roland while people streamed out for lunch, their wishes supposedly met, at least on the energetic level. I knew more about what I wished, and more about what I would do, than I had known this morning, but when Roland announced the break, Riva had ruffled Garrett's hair, smiled ruefully at me, and gone to Annie. They stood over there talking, catching up, no doubt trading congratulations on Annie's awards for condolences over Nina.

"Is it Sean?" I wasn't sure what I wanted Adela to have said.

"Didn't wake," Carlos said. "Made some sounds, moved his head. She's been praying over him."

"Good," my father said. He nodded at Roland. "You know the story?"

The wizard had been briefed about Logan at the invitation to teach. Now he said something about overlays, palimpsests, Sean standing in for Logan in Adela's mind. "What she's doing is transformative," he said. Carlos raised those eyebrows again. My father barely shrugged. I wanted Roland to ask for Riva's and my story, too, hoped he'd have something to say. But he didn't.

"Jesus fix Dad," Garrett said, curling his fingers around Roland's wrist.

"Roland isn't Jesus, Gare," my father said. "Jesus lives in heaven, with Heavenly Father. And Logan."

"Yep," said Carlos. "Though Dela doesn't think much of Heavenly Father these days." His voice trailed off.

"She's hiding out," Paul said. "She needs a blessing as much as Sean."

"So shall we go?" Roland seemed to expect that this was wanted. Every man's head nodded, Garrett's too. And mine. Total agreement. Lovely.

IN ROOM 225, GARRETT STOOD AT SEAN'S BARE FEET, RUB-bing them.

"Child reflexology," Roland murmured. "It works." We laughed, whatever ice may have formed in our fear over Sean broken. "Where do you want us to be?" the wizard asked, putting Garrett in charge. Again the boy reached for Roland's wrist and pulled him to Sean's ankle. "And the rest of us? Somebody at his head?"

"That would be Grandpa," I prompted my son, "Grandpa and Uncle Carlos." Garrett nodded. They moved into place, Carlos pulling a finger-sized phial of yellowish oil from the chest pocket of his Lodge shirt.

"What about me, then?" Adela had sat at Sean's right side all these hours, holding his drooping hand. Garrett waved, accepting and familiar. *Stay there. You need to stay right there.* Adela knuckled her eyes, a damp feathery Kleenex falling apart in her fist, but she transferred it to her lap and grasped Sean's wrist with both hands as though she would never let go.

MOUNTAIN AIR, CURRENCY OF HEALTH, BRIDGE TO VIGOR AND strength. In every season follow nature skyward: snowshoe first at the edges of snowmelt in late March to catch the pale upturning spring-beauties and woodlandstars and the hanging yellow glacier lilies. Move upfield as the snows recede; don't touch till the first blossoms peal, bright five-pointed (or eight-rayed or multidimensional) contours in colors no one could dream, shades of violet almost white, blue almost black, orange almost pink. Learn their nomenclature—poems, jokes, technical metaphors—purple monkshood and pink springbeauty at the edge of the snowmelt in April, stoneseed or pale puccoon on drier slopes in May, prince's pine or pipsissewa (say it!) in evergreen groves in late July. Snow level and elevation determine bloom times, location the blossoms themselves—near water, under stones, in meadows open to the air. For all of these hike the backcountry, folds and ridges, meadows and stands of fir or aspen, with paper and press clamps in packs on backs for hanging plaques and herb concoctions to sell in the shop. Some days, gather fallen wood (never living!) to neatly pile for winter. Other times swim, fish, visit cabin dwellers. In winter, follow rabbit tracks and weasels, observe retreats from summer haunts, withdrawals to austerity. At home—o fortunate home—kindle the lobby's great woodstove, greet guests, draw maps of the mountain's terrain to answer the newcomers' questions and nurture the property's gifts. Grow the boy strong. Ride the fluid elixir. Cease grieving the other lost children.

Until avalanche collapse the bridge, dam the flow, shear the living jewels across their faces.

Advance, demons, in droves.

AT SEAN'S HEAD, CARLOS UNSCREWED THE BLACK CAP from the consecrated oil and tilted the container so that two or three drops fell glistening on the crown of Sean's head. "Full name?"

"Sean Finn," I said.

"Sean Finn," he said, ritually addressing the afflicted, "by the power of the holy priesthood which I hold, I anoint you for a blessing ..."

The fingers of Roland's left hand gestured "come to me, come to me," gathering the vibrations of Carlos's words to his own energy. Garrett's left hand covered Roland's right, on Sean's ankle, and with his other hand, the boy grasped the top of his father's naked left foot, splayed outward, vulnerable, underneath the sheet.

"Garrett," Sean muttered.

Garrett snapped his gaze to mine. *Did you hear that?*

I did. "Go," I said. He skittered behind Roland, past Adela, wiggling his way between Carlos and Paul at the head of his father's bed. Carlos dragged one of the lightweight plastic chairs away from the room's periphery and lifted Garrett onto it so that he stood at the grown men's level. Garrett patted his father—face, shoulders, hair.

Sean craned his neck, turning his head back and forth on the pillow though his eyes remained closed.

"Oh," Adela said.

"Go on, Paul," Carlos said.

Paul said, "I—seal—this anointing upon you ..."

Roland's fingers made their "come to me" gesture again. I thought I heard the dippers that popped in the river at dawn, the muffled rustle of wind in pines and aspen. No one moved their hands from Sean's form. Swirling energy spiraled up and out from the crumpled sheets beneath him. Still Paul hesitated, could not go on. Garrett put his free hand over both of Paul's.

"You are *blessed*," Paul said in a tone I hardly recognized. He looked up and around as if he wasn't sure where he was, caught my eyes and came back to himself, speaking again, loudly this time. "You have a work to do to prove yourself. Come back and do it. I say this in the name of Jesus Christ, amen." Everyone's hands opened as if to catch these words, multiplying them over Sean, showering him with them, our collective breath held.

"Gare." Eyelids fluttering, Sean arched his neck again, reaching for something just outside his head. A sweaty half-moon trailed his hair in the flat hospital pillow. "Fish 'em in, Gare. Bringem." Or *brigham,* or *big 'un.*

"Dad!" Garrett's eyes were huge and shining.

"'Fisherman'?" Adela asked.

Paul and Carlos stepped back, to give the blessing space, I guess. Roland's right hand was raised, a satellite dish receiving and returning waves from everyone waiting, sure of the miracle about to occur. Garrett held fists of his father's hair on either temple. But there was no more movement.

"What now?" Someone's voice came out of the trance. Mine. "Good question," my father said. "Roland?"

"We don't know his time frame," Roland said, as if from a long way away. "Adela, what are you getting? Is he in there?"

"He's there," she said firmly.

"Do you want us to stay?" Carlos asked. She shook her head. Garrett climbed down from his chair, gliding his forearm across his father's form like a kind of minesweep as he came around the bed to Roland and me and holding up his arms. We wrapped ourselves around each other, his legs gripping my waist, my neck in his chokehold.

After a suitable wait, Carlos leaned down to kiss Adela. "I guess we're done," he said. "Keep watch."

"I do." She held up her hand joined to Sean's. "Finish the workshop," she said. "That's important." Roland bowed assent. So we went back to the Lodge, purified.

IV. The seeds you've sown yield up the fruit you need.

"KARMA," JEAN LUBBOCK SAID, OPENING THE AFTERNOON Q and A session. "What do you mean by that, Roland? What if your patients don't believe?" She held the hand of her sister-wife, the two of them seated on flat brown cushions, their backs against the paneled wall of the conference room, the summer sun slanting across the room over their heads to the side door where Paul had left Carlos so he could sit again with Garrett and me. Roland slurped at a peach. Annie had saved it for him from the Lodge buffet, and he wiped his fingers on a paper napkin on his lap, offering a mildly self-mocking apology for eating in front of his students. But nobody objected. They'd eaten well and were glad to have him at leisure, glad to be able to ask what was on their (our) minds: how do you do what you do? What shall we do when you're gone? It wasn't lost on me that these were questions his disciples asked Jesus—Paul made sure I knew the New Testament stories even if he suspected I'd never buy into them. But truth to tell, today I genuinely wanted to know their answers. Paul sat forward, listening too.

"Law of consequences, that's all karma is," Roland said, cryptic as ever. "You don't have to believe in it for it to be true." I saw Annie grin maternally (good answer, wizard!) from her fluffy black cushion next to Riva, who—notwithstanding she took joy in Annie—looked mournful to me, sad. Nina hadn't run back to her at the break, I guessed.

"But what if someone saddles you with pain? Is that fair?" Jean pressed. "Some consequences don't result at all from your decisions. They just come flooding in and drown you."

Roland stopped chewing. He held the dripping fruit a little way from his mouth, drying his chin and holding the napkin so it caught the pithy juice. He took two breaths, gazing at the sister-wives with a bit of a squint. Garrett lay against me, his head rolled to my left shoulder, nearly asleep.

"Will you tell me how the two of you came to join?" Roland asked, his tone conversational, his words ambiguous.

"Join what?"

"Whatever you like." Straightforward enough. "Join what brought you together. Join each other. Whatever you like."

"I'll tell him," Peggy Lubbock said. "The new and everlasting covenant."

Roland waited a beat. "Is that your answer too?"

Jean took two breaths herself, but nodded.

"A spiritual thing, then?" When both of them agreed, he asked, "What does it mean? To you?"

Paul leaned from his chair against the wall and whispered into my right ear, "He's in way over his head."

Well, maybe. Riva swore "the Principle" meant in the twenty-first century what they'd practiced in the nineteenth: polygyny, one man sealed to many women. But if you looked hard, and you looked smart in the histories, even then women were sealed to multiple men too. Everyone joined by God on earth to everyone, backward and forward in time—that was the impossible, real-time goal, which I could hardly wrap my mind around. But there was something about Roland's notions that didn't seem so far apart from that.

Garrett muttered, straightening his head underneath my lifted chin. Jean and Peggy opened their mouths to speak. Suddenly, metal screeched against metal. Keifer Lubbock, the bulky bearded anachronism of the compound at Cottonwood Canyon, threw aside the sliding door Carlos had not shut tight. He must have known exactly where his young wives sat, been listening since the break. "Don't you say a word," he said. "Get up. You're comin' with me."

Peggy howled a catlike howl while Jean shook her braid, defiant, an arm flung across her sister-wife's body in support and declaration. Riva scrambled toward them. Garrett, startled, pushed himself against me awkwardly to see what woke him. Every other participant froze.

Roland raised an assertive hand. "Excuse us," he said. "We're doing specific healing work here. We invite you to stay, but not to disrupt."

"I ain't disrupting nothin'," Lubbock said, leaning to yank at Peggy's shoulder, his grip a harshness beside the brace. "I'm taking my women home."

Peggy jerked away. He shifted his fist to the brace itself. Everyone sucked in their breath.

"Lubbock." My father had come to his feet without my seeing. "You've got a restraining order," he said calmly. How did he know? "There's a lawyer in the house. Shall I get him?"

Riva stood now just outside the Lubbock war zone, one arm raised to match Roland's. I imagined fierce protection flying back and forth, royal and crimson, between the energy wielders. Peggy Lubbock clung to Riva's leg from the floor. Her apparatus kept her from collapsing as she seemed to want to do, and I felt Garrett clutching me as if in sympathy, but harder, if that were possible, his gasp and rigid spine his own version of the brace—the awful preface to a seizure.

"Son?" He couldn't speak. It was the old pattern—squinched-shut eyes, dithered tongue, a detached consciousness arming itself for battle against my boy.

"Help!" someone called. It could have been anyone—Peggy, Riva, Paul, Roland—but of course it was me. *This has everything to do with you!* Noise of a scuffle drowned out fragments of directions in Paul's or Roland's voice. Footsteps clattered past us, a sliding door rumbled shut. When I looked up, Keifer Lubbock, Peggy, and my father were gone, a daunting combination. Roland flew to us, arms extended. I grabbed one of them. "Hold him while I get his herbs," I said.

Roland gripped my fingers with one hand, but with the other, he arranged Garrett's body, his clothes, made him comfortable. "Send healing where it's needed—I'll help." I broke open the little ampule I kept in my jacket pocket, slipped it under Garrett's tongue, then clapped one hand on my son's forehead, the other on his chest—not mystical decisions, simply the closest and most convenient spots. Roland covered my shaking hands with his. Palpable vibrations intersected me; we focused our pooled knowledge on my boy.

SINKING TO THE BOTTOM OF THE LAKE, DESPERATE FOR AIR, the life-hold lost for good to inches then yards of watery space, the child sees the anchor arm recede through bubbling breath-line backward to the surface. Ah, there's no point in opening or closing the mouth to cry out or to call, but there in the current hovers a circle of helpers, mother after rippling mother, white-haired and horizontally tall, full-breasted and smiling peacefully, or open-mouthed as if singing, dark braids drifting, children in their arms waving graceful little hands. Yet others, not all women, familiar, fin-like, bob further and nearer, nearer and further, extending themselves, floating with and beneath the child, holding place, stilling the turbulent lungs and heart, calling "you, lovely, keep living, no leaving," a frothy enticement beckoning back from the deep till suddenly breath returns—

GARRETT COUGHED, GAGGED, GASPED. "FISHERMAN!" HE squeezed Roland's fingers in his fist, his bottom digging a crater in my cross-legged lap, his head crushing my breastbone. "Him! Fish!" *Lubbock?* Was that who Sean meant? Did Garrett know what Lubbock was about? I dove inside, where the mothers were, and they nodded.

AFTERWARD, WE HAD THE SENSE THAT SOMEBODY DIRECTED. No one had to say, but Riva stayed with Annie at the workshop, devising on the spot a closing sequence for the class. They told later how change flashed through the room, stunning some participants and sending others into bliss and making others strong where they'd been powerless before. Roland, for his part, gathered Garrett to his chest, storming after Paul in the assumption I'd stay with him every step. It's possible there were clues, muddy footprints or half-open doorways in the hall between the workshop room and the lobby of the Lodge, but I remain convinced that the mothers, Adela and the ones from underneath the lake, drew a lucent line for us to follow, tracing where we had to go, between the glass-topped tables in the foyer with their wildflower vases and oak-burl lamps, down the front steps in a zigzag and across the parking lot where Sean was felled the night before. Halfway down, Carlos joined the fray, grunting his shock and support as Keifer, astonishingly lithe in flight, kitty-cornered the Beamers and Jeeps on the cobblestone and angled down the steep front garden, leafy now with late-summer toadflax and lupine, toward the river's rock-coursed banks. Paul—smaller, fitter, barely missing his quarry's flapping jacket—stayed ahead of Carlos, and we three panted hard behind.

Finally, Carlos had to stop, hands on knees, wheezing. "The shed! Go on!"

The shed was the toolhouse, repository of rakes and trowels, hoses and shears and Adela's flower presses, clamped and boarded now with blossoms drying since the spring. Sure enough, the beeline led to there, though why we'd no idea. The goldenrod surrounding the shed went down under Lubbock's feet. We could barely see his head and shoulders ducking through the brush, but the woody crackling stems left a trail for Paul to track. Roland hoisted Garrett to his back—an easier tromp—and the boy let a grin split through the fear as he twined arms around the wizard's neck. I managed a rub, a pat, before we were off again. Carlos came after. Thirty yards and we caught up to the face-off.

It was like a bear fight. Keifer snarled and hollered, keeping Paul away with the force of his wildness. When he saw us coming up behind, he roared as if in triumph.

"There he is," he bellowed, "you brought'm to me, let me at 'im!" He lunged past Paul, throwing my father aside (though Paul didn't stumble, kept himself upright), clawing at Roland— not for the healer himself but for the boy on his back.

I threw myself at Lubbock, unbalancing him just long enough for Roland to hurl Garrett into Carlos's waiting arms. I staggered sideways, skimming Lubbock's ribs, and his elbow slammed my skull so I saw spots and lost my legs. Not for long—I scrambled back to vision, pummeling, but he abandoned me for Roland, or no, for Carlos—no, for Garrett. "His father killed our Leeny! Blood atonement! Vengeance eternal!"

Roland, arm outflung against the adversary, stopped fully for a second to stare his question at me: *Blood atonement?* I drew a finger fast across my neck to demonstrate the ancient and extreme belief—"blood spilt upon the ground, that smoke thereof might counter evil sins"—and though I felt impervious, infused with power, I knew the fanatic meant it. Paul picked his way through goldenrod to muster at his rear—my father's courage swelled my heart—and Roland, stumbling on the uneven earth to Carlos, held up both arms, a display of sheer ferocity. Then behind me I heard women.

Peggy was at their head. Riva, Jean, and Annie flanked her, a phalanx of Amazons come to wage a war. Peggy reached up to her neck brace, arms flashing white, unfastening the Velcro strips that held the splint in place. She unwound it and flung it into the weeds, oblivious to her sweater snagged on thistles, her ankles turned on hillocky ground. Behind her, the sun slid past the highest peak so that her dangling hair glowed, a halo lit by holy fire.

"I hereby break our seal, Keifer Lubbock!" Her voice throbbed— a function of the bowl-shaped drainage, or of her thorough transformation. "I'll be alone in heaven before I'll go with you!"

Stupefied, he turned toward her voice, but like a blinded beast swung back his head to Carlos, attention caught by Roland's double force—his own and Garrett's energy, fused and flowing. "What lies you telling Peg?"

Like a circle of warriors, we all took steps toward the man, closing in, shutting him off. Unhinged, he sprang, and Roland sidestepped, loosening Garrett in a tumble. Lubbock snatched at Garrett's jacket as he had at Peggy's, and in two strides had knocked Roland aside and locked himself and Garrett in the shed.

I was far away and far too close at once. An engine throbbed behind me in the parking lot. I could hear breathing, and the scraping of Peggy's shoes as she approached, and the muffled rustle of wind in pines and aspen. But the center and circumference of everything was my son inside the shed.

Peggy stood exalted, taking stock of her own changes, and Riva with her. Whatever mobilized the rest of us let them have their moment, but as for us, we were a battalion with a purpose. Carlos knew the shed, of course, and so did I (though not as well). He tossed keys at my father and met me at the side, where through the window we could see presses rising in stacks. Roland and Paul knelt at the door around the corner. Paul had his mobile phone out and called a warning—"We're bringing in the law! Come out while you still can!" I saw Roland raise his palms, flashing energy everywhere. I *knew* it helped, felt power flood my breast, though that seemed as crazy a notion as blood atonement or anything else we'd done or heard so far. My father found the key at second try and rattled at the door. But Lubbock must have been inside, pulling—the door didn't budge.

We scrambled for a rock to break the window. Annie—how did she know? But why did I question?—appeared from nowhere, lugging a stone the size of my head in her weighted arms. "Think of it as everything we're changing," she said as she heaved. Glass cracked and clattered, and presses tottered inward. His jacket sleeve around his fist, Carlos cleared the frame. He couldn't pull himself over the sill, though, so he picked me up and Annie helped him thread me through.

Yes, I cut myself. I still show the trophy scars in my calf and knee. But I heard Garrett grunting syllables and knew precisely where to go. From the dim corner I could see my son, wedged between a hose-snake and the door, Lubbock's beefy arm shoving his face aside so that he couldn't cry out for help.

Presses for flowers require C-clamps with screws to hold the plywood layers tighter as the blossoms dry. In the shed, the presses were piled so deep, so many boards between, that the screws with their turnkeys leaned out into the space like pitchforks in a field. I couldn't lift the presses, but if Paul and Carlos could distract the enemy, with the screws I could devise some harm from here.

Lubbock bore down upon the door, blustering like wind on angry seas. On the other side of his hold, Jean had joined the men. I could hear her soothing, though I couldn't make out words, and now he quieted enough to listen. He hated what he heard. Back stiffened, he snarled expletives, tightening his hold on my son.

Who, for his part, held up. He could see my every move from the corner of one eye, squinched beneath the grip of his captor. His brain may have been damaged at birth, but it was never dull, and now he knew, by the same signs that led us all, that he must not let on he saw me. By force of miracle—Roland's hands, or mine—not a mote of him was seizing. I put a finger to my lips and knew he understood.

To thread a screw is easy without stress, mechanical or otherwise. I tried turning the levers first clockwise and then counter-, but the presses toppled against each other so the screws couldn't spiral either way, and Carlos and Annie scrabbled at the window, trying unsuccessfully for purchase. At another entreaty from Jean (and a rattle of the door from Paul), Lubbock twisted my boy's arm as I was trying to twist the screws. My neck strained with the effort, and my eyes pinched shut.

It was then I saw the mothers—there, behind my eyes. They wore their clothes like robes and radiated lore, facts I needed, stories in images of suffering, of choosing—life, and death. Love, too. This had everything to do with me, and I knew why, and what to do. I raised my lids, and one and then another and another clamp unwound and lifted off a press that sat just so against the wall. Gravity helped me lay the plywood gently on the floor. The papers, drying arrowleaf, slid whispering between.

I held the three big clamps for Gare to see. Carlos told me later he saw them from the window, too—they looked like spears, he said, or tomahawks, silhouetted as they were in brightness (the sun was on the door side of the shed, sinking with the afternoon). Something caught Lubbock's hearing, so he spun, keeping his shoulder at the door, grinding his fist against Garrett's throat, a trapped and crazy man strangling my boy. I held the clamp-screws out before me like war clubs and caterwauled as I charged. Lubbock took a screw-head in the stomach and doubled over, thundering, letting go of the door so that Paul fell inside. I rolled aside. Garrett crawled out of Lubbock's grip and hunched behind the door, opposite the men from me. As Paul and Lubbock fought, Roland whirled magnificently around the door to be with Garrett. Lubbock smashed the door against him, and he fell. I heard metal clatter, Garrett yelled, and there he was, my son, on his feet, a pair of shears raised high above his head, waiting for nothing. Lubbock's feet blundered in the dust, motes flashing in the last moments of light—Garrett saw his chance—the shears slashed the soft tissue behind the fundamentalist's ankle and again into the top of the foot. Blood spurted and pooled. Lubbock roared and toppled like a mast in a storm at sea, and Roland and Paul were upon him as we heard sirens and Carlos fell, panting, through the window.

V ... till your partner has her wish and so do you.

EVERYONE WAS IMPLICATED. IT SEEMED IMPOSSIBLE THAT the workshop should continue, the Festival go on. But Lubbock wasn't mortally hurt, and Roland said (and I believed him, while my father laughed in dazed relief) that Garrett's aura was five times more radiant than normal, clarified and bright. The sheriff's men took notes, shook Garrett's hand, stove Lubbock in their chicken-wired wagon, and mopped the bloody floorboards, so though some of the crowd drifted away, strained beyond capacity to meditate or ponder, enough stayed that the wizard agreed, bemused, to teach another piece. "For closure," he said, then, punning, "we're all mortgaged to this afternoon— by fate, or karma, or belief." That made me shiver. I sat aside again with Paul, who kept one hand protectively on Garrett, who shimmered in my lap.

To Peggy it was like a carnival, I guess. She glowed, too, like Garrett, and though Jean did not—I imagined she anticipated only too clearly certain trials to come, with or without Keifer— still, the two of them were joined at hand and hip and waited like one person for Roland's last advice. Riva and Annie also clustered close, their heads bent, murmuring. I didn't want to hear what they were saying. Carlos checked in again on Dela with our news. Hers was that Sean felt different through her hands, though his breathing hadn't changed "You should spell her tonight," he told me. "I'll switch you at the reading." "Fine with me," I said. I had no need to watch The Annie Show. So there we were, adrenaline and disbelief receding, the sun a fading disk behind the mountain while the wizard made his ploy.

YOU, YOURSELF, ARE THE INSTRUMENT OF HEALING. Don't fool yourself. It isn't personal, this power you have. It's the opposite of ego, a calling, a force requiring of you forgiveness for the human thing you are.

Think of it: beginning healers learn mechanics, steps of processes repeated and embellished with each generation's grace. The more advanced recruit their consciousness to influence and guide. Master healers, though—disciples with commitment— they don't 'fix.' They create within themselves conditions for new choice, and offer up their lives.

Any of us can do it. But few have sufficient courage.

PAUL WATCHED THE STUDENTS PAIR AND WEAVE THEIR energetic charms, arms waving or hovering over each other's hearts or heads or backs. He leaned to me. "Have you done that?" he said.

"It seems to work," I said.

"Don't you know we have the priesthood?" We weren't fighting. He was genuinely curious, concerned. He'd taught me all he could, those single-father years of Sunday School and prayer. This energetic work had resonance and light. It echoed what he knew, but wasn't *it.*

What was? Adela in the room with Sean? The mothers, pulling me to shore? Garrett, touched and changed by fishers on the mount?

Which reminded me.

"Gare," I whispered, while Roland's people trembled in their places, giving and receiving forgiveness and new voice.

"Mom?" I loved that he could speak.

"Tell me if the bad man at the shed was the fisherman he meant, your dad, back there in the hospital room."

He nodded solemnly, then pulled my ear to his lips, his hands steady and strong. "Curse words," he whispered. "Dad said"—he lifted up one of those hands—"'Jesus.'"

"Like that? His hand up? 'Jesus'?" Paul heard and joined his head to ours.

"Sean drove Lubbock off last night in Jesus's name," I said. Garrett nodded eagerly. I'd got it.

"Did that make Lubbock mad?" My father searched, as I did, for connections—had Lubbock caused Sean's wound? Garrett hid his face inside my shirt.

"Gare," I said, pulling him back, "you're not a baby any more. You have to tell us. What happened then?"

"I forgot," he said. Brave. "Now I 'member. Fish'm'n hit Dad. Then ran away."

"Damn," Paul said.

"Blood atonement," I said. "Sean got Garrett home. Then collapsed below."

My father looked distraught. So much injustice! That wickedness could multiply itself and father-forth—

"Well, he's in custody now," I said. "There's nothing we can do."

Still my father shook his head.

Stirrings in the room indicated that the workshop task was done. Roland thanked everyone, recommended Annie's reading, promised wrap-up in the morning. People clustered, hugged, retreated. Within minutes there were only us and Roland, Riva, Annie, Peggy. Even Jean was gone. The three women spoke briefly to Roland, then went aside, deciding pre-show plans. Roland came again to us. It touched me how he remembered. This time, he knelt beside Paul, one hand on his back, the other on his knee. "Would you like some stomach assistance?"

Paul grinned a skeptic's welcome. "How'd you know?"

"Oh, I can see," the wizard said. "Come on, we'll let the master help." He pulled Garrett off my lap. "Sit close," he said, settling the boy on his grandpa's lap. "Love his tummy." He took my hand in his (*oh, keep it there forever!*) and laid it atop Garrett's. Those hands hummed, they sang, they vibrated a chord. I felt Riva and Annie observe, and didn't mind. Let them watch. My father bowed his head. I knew he prayed, and knew it couldn't hurt. I caught Garrett's eye. He smiled and winked. He *winked.* Surely we would be all right.

About the Author

JULIE J. NICHOLS GREW UP IN THE San Francisco Bay Area. She lives now with her husband, Nick, in Provo, Utah, where they raised their four excellent children and myriad animals. She has, in her lifetime, been Associate Professor of creative writing at Utah Valley University, energy healer, Relief Society president and Gospel Doctrine teacher, reviewer of books for *Publishers Weekly* and other venues, and besotted grandma, though not all at the same time and not all with the same enthusiasm. She extends thanks to everyone whose encouragement and expertise contributed to this book. She is at work on another novel. She can be reached at nicholju@uvu.edu.

Photo credit: Jessie Eyre

Made in the USA
Lexington, KY
04 October 2016

FICTION

These stories trace the arc of a family narrative in which
their children for the best of reasons, fierce daughters re
and the gap between spiritual health and the expectation
affects the outcome of every episode.

Poet Annie MacDougal, feminist Riva Maynard, and Riva's daughter Katie spiral
in and out of these seven "incidents" spanning more than three decades, along
with the men and women they learn from and love.

"Just as God's eye is on the sparrow, Julie Nichols's clear-sighted, penetrating eye is on the lives of Mormon women and men and our yearnings and
shortcomings."

—Joanna Brooks, *Book of Mormon Girl*

"These linked stories . . . are consistently faithful and questioning, intelligent
and spiritual, essentially Mormon and essentially inclusive of those who
inhabit the fringe."

—John Bennion, *Falling Toward Heaven*

"In this intricately patterned collection, [Nichols] addresses the violence,
mystery, and most of all the messy beauty of marriage, motherhood, love, and
forgiveness in a lush, lyrical prose which honours the magical in the everyday."

—Jenn Ashworth, *The Friday Gospels*

ZARAHEMLA
BOOKS

ZarahemlaBooks.com